# THE MATTER

## STEPHANIE PERCIVAL

Cinnamon Press
:: small miracles from distinctive voices ::

Published by Cinnamon Press
Meirion House
Tanygrisiau
Blaenau Ffestiniog
Gwynedd LL41 3SU
www.cinnamonpress.com
The right of Stephanie Percival to be identified as author of this work has
been asserted by her in accordance with the Copyright, Designs and Patent
Act, 1988. © 2019 Stephanie Percival. ISBN 978-1-78864-040-4
Designed and typeset in Garamond by Cinnamon Press. Cover design by
Adam Craig © Adam Craig.
Cinnamon Press is represented by Inpress and by the Welsh Books Council
in Wales. Printed in Poland.
The publisher acknowledges the support of the Welsh Books Council.

## Acknowledgements

In early 2015, I attended one of the inspiring Writers' retreats in North
Wales, led by Jan Fortune of Cinnamon Press. I took the first pages of
'the matter' for a feedback session. The reaction from the other writers
was positive…Thanks for that! Also Jan liked it and, at that early stage,
said she would publish it once finished. Thanks Jan, for your belief,
support and for keeping your promise.

A Big Thank you to all of the Cinnamon Press team, and if you love
the cover design as much as I do…that's down to Adam Craig. Thanks
Adam.

My family and friends have supported me with my writing from the
start. So Thanks go to all of you, and to everybody who has read my
work and given encouragement and feedback… It makes all the
difference.

You can connect with Stephanie on Facebook: StephaniePercival—
Author, or on her website: www.stephaniepercival.com

the matter

# I

Imagine, if you will, a clenched fist. And as the fingers unfurl an object is revealed. It looks like a hand grenade and indeed it is about to explode. This is a metaphor for the creation of the universe. The beginning... The Big Bang. Now we must ask, to whom does the metaphorical fist belong? I suggest an entity of energy, no face, no speech. Perhaps if you have a mathematical brain you might consider it another dimension but if you are a story-teller you might give it a form similar to a human or you might want to call it God. That is entirely up to you. For the purposes of this narrative it will be termed 'entity'.

Now imagine another fist. This is also clenched but it is made of skin and bone and blood vessels, and is recognisable as a man's hand. In it is a pebble picked from a jungle floor. The fist belongs to Professor Ambrose Isherwood. Ambrose is wishing he were explaining the beginning of the universe to his child rather than the group of strangers surrounding him. Or perhaps he should just give in and head back to his real work, trying to discover subatomic particles under the Yorkshire hills.

Slowly he unfurls his fist and says, 'The universe started as a small object of huge density, then at the Big Bang it expanded into the universe we know today.'

'Wow, that's amazin' Rambo,' a blonde actress says, touching his hand. He cringes at the touch and winces at the moniker he has been given since he wore a bandana for one of the challenges. He is more used to being addressed as Professor or Sir, but realises he is now part of a world, a microcosm, where they speak another language and have different rules of engagement. For the first time since landing in the 'Celeb Jungle' he is feeling his age.

Ambrose avoids tabloids, which describe him as 'the silver fox of science'. But the strapline is difficult to escape. He is the most popular scientist of the day, renowned for his energetic and daring style of presentation while rock climbing or scuba diving; carrying out experiments on his blood or lung capacity, sticking needles into himself while skydiving or motor racing.

'How can summat like that become the whole universe?' Mallory continues. Her fingers remain on his arm. She is barefoot and, even though he is six foot tall, she looms above him.

When Ambrose does these promotional stunts he sometimes questions how he ended up here, pandering to celeb culture. He ponders how in thousands of years *Homo sapiens* has developed technology such as TV and computers and satellites, the ability to travel quickly across the globe and into space and yet most humans have not got much further than survival and pleasure-seeking.

The other thing about this particular scenario is that it is completely contrived, a little snippet dreamed up by the production team. He feels more like a rat in someone else's experiment each day, and longs for home and his own research project.

Ambrose sighs, he is having difficulty concentrating. He is aware of Mallory's enhanced breasts bulging from the skimpy bikini. He suspects Mallory and several of the others have had botox because, though they are all younger than his sixty-four years, their expressions don't change. It is like being circled by a gang of zombies.

He takes a breath and continues, 'It comes down to the way the universe behaves today; it follows the laws of quantum mechanics and relativity. E equals m, c squared. You've heard of that haven't you?'

There are some shakes of the head. He looks at the blank, beautiful faces watching him. Either they don't know or nobody is going to own up to being a swot. Ambrose sighs and looks at the stone in his palm. There is a rime of dirt under his fingernails. This does not bother him, he has been in much worse situations physically; grimier, in pain, in peril even. It is his mental state that has never been so troubled. He smoothes the pebble in his hand, imagining its atomic construction and wishes he was at home.

On the other side of the globe; his wife, Kate, is also having a difficult day. She is trying to get her son ready before she goes to work.

'Come on, Simeon,' she says, trying not to shout. Her fist is clenched around the handle of a toddler spoon, trying to get porridge in to Simeon's mouth. But every time it gets near he flails an arm and jerks his head. Simeon is eleven and confined in a specialised chair, with straps to hold his body still. Mostly, he keeps his eyes closed, when he opens them there are shapes and figures that swim at him in a blur. He is not conscious of the food, just that something is being pushed at him. 'Simeon. Please come on. I'm going to be late.' Simeon hears the words but does not connect with them... In his head is just white noise, which moves around. Sometimes it becomes unbearable in its intensity making him react physically, and at other times it is a gentle lapping. For a short while everything had been going too fast, the noise accompanied by flashing images rushing through his brain. So he screams.

Kate feels the urge to scream too but she draws in a deep breath and mutters 'patience, patience.' She knows that the more anxious she is, the more unsettled Simeon becomes but, even after eleven years, she finds it difficult.

'Simeon, please,' says Kate, putting the spoon down and wiping Simeon's face with a moist cloth.

He does not understand time, the need for hurry. And if he screams, the rushing around him usually slows. Then things return to their natural rhythm, one his body can accommodate...

'Where the hell is Marietta?' asks Kate to herself. 'Marietta!' she calls, in the vain hope that the child minder has arrived.

Marietta is kneeling in a church about a mile from the Isherwood residence. Her hands are not clenched but pressed together in prayer. Entwined between her fingers is a chain of beads. Marietta has her eyes tightly shut as she prays. Her prayer, before she goes to work, is always the same, that Jesus should help the boy she cares for. 'I know it is your will, Father,' she murmurs, 'But please, in your everlasting power, help little Simeon.' The beads between her fingers have become warm. They feel heavier as she prays as if the words bind with them, concentrating her plea. She loves the church at this time in the morning; the scent of incense still lingers and makes the air heavy with a holy presence. When she opens her eyes she sees the light shine through the stained glass in coloured bands. Dust motes swirl in the air and between those bands in the shadow she thinks she can see the finger of God pointing at her. She would usually light a candle but she does not have time this morning. Mrs Isherwood doesn't want to be late to work; she has been held up several times already this month. Marietta has said she will get to the Isherwood House early. She thinks it unlikely it will make a difference to Kate leaving on time, some untoward occurrence always intervenes. Marietta genuflects, crosses herself and then hurries outside. Her sensible shoes pat-pat across the tiles on her way out. She pulls her headscarf more tightly around her head and makes her way up the hill.

Marietta enters the house by the back door into what was called the gunroom, not that it has seen a gun for many years. She hangs up her coat and changes into her indoor shoes.

She comes into the kitchen smiling and efficient, ready to do her day's work. Thanking God for keeping her busy, after all, 'Idle hands do the Devil's work.'

'Good morning, Mrs Isherwood,' she greets Kate, hardly acknowledging her presence, her attention already focused entirely on the screaming child. 'Now what's the matter, my little man?' she coos at Simeon and her gentle tone does seem to have an effect as he stops screaming and whimpers instead.

Marietta always thinks Mrs Isherwood looks tired. She is attractive for her age but her eyes are a little odd, one wide and open and the other with a squint. Marietta thinks this a result of looking down microscopes for too many years. To her it seems a very odd choice of career. She knows Kate works for a research lab, which has something to do with genetic investigation, while Ambrose is searching for some sort of 'God particle'. But who needs to know how people are put together or how the world was created, when in truth everybody knows in their heart that God is responsible for the wonders of creation. She has a children's Bible that she used to read to her own daughter and now she reads to Simeon. But she always waits until Kate has gone to work.

'Shall I take over?' Marietta asks holding her hand out for the bowl and spoon. Kate relinquishes them, not with the relief she might have expected but with a resignation that she really isn't up to the job of motherhood.

'You're too old to be a mother!' her own mother had told her when Kate announced her pregnancy. 'You should have considered your biological clock before now. It's completely selfish. Just think how old you'll be when he's twenty. You and Ambrose will be dead before he's even lived half his life.' And when Simeon was born with a genetic disorder she could sense her mother's desperate urge to say, 'I told you so.'

Today Kate feels old. She sighs as she changes her blouse, soiled with porridge from Simeon's breakfast. She finds it increasingly difficult to make even the most basic decisions these days. She had taken time to choose her first outfit and is now unsettled by the change. She looks critically at herself in the mirror, noticing only lines and flabby flesh, the roll of fat along the top of her waist-band, the drooping boobs and wrinkled skin at her throat. This year will mark her fiftieth birthday; she can't bring herself to say 'celebrate'. It feels as if she's climbing an Escher staircase, endlessly trudging around, getting nowhere except older. She doesn't like it when Ambrose is away, and now he seems to be away more and more. That is the nature of marrying a celebrity scientist. She shrugs, and pushes a strand of grey hair behind her ear, regretting she has not had time to have it coloured.

Anyway, there is never enough time in her day. She is either getting Simeon up or preparing him for bed or waking up at night to check on him or getting herself ready for meetings or trying to read a journal to keep up-to-date with the latest research or filling in forms or talking to carers or people on phones, arranging appointments...

She goes back downstairs to find Simeon eating his breakfast quite calmly.

Simeon likes the smell in the air. It is heavy and woody. Incense clings to Marietta's clothes and hair; it envelops her... He does not know the smell emanates from Marietta but is aware of the fragrance wafting about when she is present. It tickles his nose and makes him laugh. When he opens his eyes he sees an expanse of blue. It washes over his vision like a wave. Marietta likes the colour, which she associates with 'Our Lady'. She has a full palette of blue garments in her wardrobe. Today she wears a sapphire blouse and navy trousers... A crucifix hangs over her bosom and turns in the light. Simeon sees it glimmer and tries to grab at it. As usual his co-ordination is off, so it is simply a wave in the air.

'What is it you see, little one?' Marietta asks.

Kate watches the pair from the door; they look like a painted scene in a frame, one she is excluded from. Marietta must sense her hovering because she speaks to her without turning.

'Did you see Mr Isherwood on the television last night?' Then she changes the tone of her voice and speaks to Simeon, 'Did you see your Daddy on the TV, he looks so handsome. He is so clever.'

Simeon does not answer; he does not understand the question or recognise the words TV or Daddy. Other things occupy his thoughts. He is chasing specks across the spaces in his brain. He can appreciate the restriction of his harness and without it senses his body would lift and blend with the shadows around him.

Kate is glad for the interruption of the grandfather clock in the hall chiming eight. She is already late.

She doesn't tell Marietta that she watched and recorded the programme and then re-watched it, fast-forwarding it to every frame with Ambrose in. It briefly made her feel closer to him. But when she finally switched off and went to bed, the expanse of uninhabited mattress was too large without the bulk of Ambrose beside her, and she couldn't sleep.

She hardly sees Ambrose, and now he is in a jungle flirting with models and actresses half his age. Sometimes she even jokes with him that asking questions during a Q & A session after one of his lectures is the only time they speak. It is one of those jokes which is becoming too close to the truth to be amusing.

Kate gives Simeon a kiss before she leaves. 'Bye, sweetheart,' she says, 'Sorry, I've got to rush.' Simeon is sometimes aware of the hurry around him. Figures outlined in blurred brightness like films taken on long exposure. The other familiar figure is Marietta. He likes feeling her hand on his forehead and her calmer presence, as if she is in rhythm with his breathing... He sometimes says, 'Mmm,' which Marietta likes to think she taught him. Kate is sure he is trying to say 'Mummy.' In fact, it means nothing, but is all the sound, beside a scream, that Simeon can make. And it is a comforting sound as he vibrates the air on his lips.

# II

The entity existed before everything. Before nothing. It moves as entities can through time and space; immortal, invisible. Although present within the Universe it has created, it remains at a distance like a shadow hovering. It has no concept of the sort of time humanity has invented. The sort of time that equations are made of.

As Kate drives to the research institute she is not aware of anything other than the road and buildings she drives past each day. They have become so familiar that they are an unseen backdrop. She does not switch the radio on as she sometimes does; today she wants a little space, a pause from the anxiety at home and the bustle of the lab.

Her pause is all too brief. The red and white barrier to the car park looms ahead of her. She winds the window down and slots her pass into the automated machine.

Then her usual routine of entering the modern lab block, a good morning to Barry at reception and up in the elevator to the third floor.

Her office is a small space she shares with three others. It is still cluttered with old office furniture and filing cabinets, which have yet to be replaced years after the transfer to the modern research building. On her desk, just visible behind a stack of papers, is a dusty frame. It holds a photo of Simeon, age four, with Ambrose. Simeon is smiling as usual.

Kate puts her briefcase on the desk, causing a cascade on the computer keyboard, the monitor and the papers, so the frame gets pushed into the wall and is completely obscured. Kate does not notice.

She switches the computer on to check her emails, expecting the usual mass of unnecessary correspondence. Her attention is taken by a red exclamation mark against a message from her manager, Kamir Mehta. It is a summons to a meeting at 2 o'clock, in his office. There is no pleasantry or information about the demand, all she can do is wait and fret. It has gone half past eight and she is late again. She chews a fingernail, wondering how often in the last month she has not been on time. Now all she can think of is the meeting. She swivels her chair around so she can look out of the window. From here on the edges of the city she can glimpse the towers of York Minster; it has a solidity about it. Since Roman times, when the city was called Eboracum, a central place of gathering has existed, parts of which remain below the Minster. That, she muses is the nature of things; layer upon layer, ever changing and yet the essence remaining the same.

She knows she should get on with the latest project but feels numbed by the potential warning she is going to receive from Kamir. She swings the chair from side to side, in a motion which counts down towards 2 o'clock. The second hand clicks by slowly. Even if she swivels the chair faster, time does not speed up. She has to wait.

'Hi, Kate.' A voice from the open doorway. It takes a moment for Kate to stir from her reverie and swing the chair around. Carol, a research colleague from the University, comes in holding a beaker from the vending machine. 'Can I get you a coffee?' she asks.

'No, thanks.' Kate is worried about upsetting her digestion before her meeting. She wishes she could close the office door against her colleagues today, rather than leave it wide open in the usual invitation for anybody to wander in. She likes Carol, they are of a similar age and background. But Kate is aware of a drop in her stomach, a sensation she always experiences when they meet, as if something has been pushed over the edge of a high tower. A sense of loss. Carol has two children, a boy and a girl, older than Simeon and both at University. A future Simeon can never experience.

'Never mind, I can see you've a lot on your mind this morning,' Carol says, smiling, then turns and leaves the room.

'Thanks,' Kate responds, then wonders if Carol has heard something on the grapevine.

She manages to review her emails again, skimming most of them. She puts on her white coat and goes into the lab to see what task she should be doing today. A whiteboard, gridded with red pen in wobbly lines, tells her where she should be. She is glad of the guidance, her own motivation is lacking. Lights blink on the bank of computerised equipment; they give the impression of problems being methodically worked through. She settles on a stool in front of her workbench. Other colleagues are already busy measuring and recording things, reading data on screens or pipetting liquid into racks of test tubes. One or two look up and nod in her direction but quickly turn away again. Kate becomes certain they know of her forthcoming interview.

She is not sure how she gets through the morning and brief lunch break. She has forgotten any data she has recorded. It simply blurs into a series of numbers and equations with no meaning and no consequence. It won't matter if she is fired.


Finally 2 o'clock comes. She arrives promptly and knocks on the door. There is an ominous one-word invitation from Kamir. 'Come!'

She is surprised by the cheery greeting that follows.

'Welcome, Kate. How's Ambrose getting on? So, he's in the celebrity jungle then?' Before she can reply he has already continued, 'Can't stand the programme myself.'

Kate's mind is a blur; she doesn't want to have a chat with Kamir Mehta, she wants him to get to the point. But he has always appeared far more interested in her successful husband than her. She respects him but has never really liked him. He is continuing to give his view on reality television but she is only watching his jaw move. She decides it is too symmetrical like a cartoon character and the goatee beard is overly trimmed as if he might have some geometric tool for measuring its exact dimensions. He always treats everybody pleasantly but Kate imagines he never gives others much thought because he is so full of himself. Perhaps that's why he remains a bachelor in his forties. However, she has to admit that otherwise Kamir Mehta is an excellent Departmental Head. He is the most calm and organised scientist Kate has ever met. Every problem is thought through and dealt with in a logical manner, whether it is a scientific conundrum or simply one of cigarette butts dropped in the car park.

'Kate,' she finally hears, 'Kate,' he repeats, 'I suspect you must be wondering why I invited you here?'

Kate nods. He is being far too relaxed if he is about to give her a warning. He has a cheesy smile, revealing his even white teeth; they glint like an advertisement for toothpaste.

'Well, this is a very sensitive matter, and I need you to know that what I'm going to tell you is hush-hush, and not to be discussed with anybody else at this time.' He leans forward, stroking a strand of dark hair back into its gelled perfection. Kate can smell the citrus of the product.

She senses her forehead frowning. She is becoming more and more confused. She has always suspected Kamir might be a game player but had never considered that she would be involved. She continues to nod.

'The fact is, our research with the genetic engineering programme has reached a very delicate stage. As you know we're getting very close to clinical trials. And you know from our research, those on mammals have been very positive.'

He pauses for a moment, scans the tinted windows, appraising his reflection and then continues. 'It's just that I can't get the go ahead from the board for human trials.'

There is a longer pause in which Kate thinks she can hear the synaptic connections fizz in her brain. Is he going to suggest what she thinks he is going to suggest? This has happened before. In a minute he will toss a paper clip in the air.

'If we had a willing subject, I think we could by-pass some of the red tape. Of course, it is completely irregular, but think what we'd achieve if it were successful.'

There is another pause. Kate hasn't studied Kamir's eyes before but the intensity of the dark brown, almost burnished quality of the irises seems to scorch her skin. He is fiddling with a paper-clip on his desk. She can't speak but watches his manicured fingers turn the bent metal over and over.

'You have a son, yes?'

She whispers the name, 'Simeon.'

'Yes, Simon. And he has Angelman Syndrome?'

'Similar to that,' again her response is barely audible.

'The positive thing about Angelman Syndrome is that it is a one-gene mutation. Something we are ready to trial. Perhaps we can help Simon. He can be our first success; our moon landing, our giant leap for mankind. It will change history. And it will be Simon who is the star.'

Kamir leans back in his chair and then flicks the paperclip upwards. It glints as it arcs in the air and lands on the carpet near Kate's shoe. She follows it with her eyes and notices a ladder in her tights.

'This is obviously a momentous decision for you Kate, one you need to discuss with Ambrose and nobody else. Take some time out today and get back to me... Let me know if there is a possibility of going ahead? Shall we say by the end of June?'

Kate can hear as well as feel her heart beat as she walks down the central corridor. The white walls intensify the pulsing. She wonders whether she is having a breakdown and is in a white-walled specialist unit somewhere. She

16

imagines she has experienced her conversation with Kamir before, not a passing sensation like déjà-vu, but as if she has lived this episode in a dream state. Somehow she has known this event was going to happen.

Returning to her office she sees all the commonplace things of her working life. The computers, the piled-up papers. Her briefcase is where it should be. The only oddness is that she sees no one.

Kate is still shaking as she reverses out of the parking place. She still cannot comprehend the conversation with Kamir. She can't go home yet. It is too early in the afternoon, so she drives around the city by-pass for a time and then stops in a lay-by. She watches cows wander across a field, chewing the cud as if this were a very ordinary day.

# III

Can an entity have offspring? Well, this entity does. But the infant is not strong. It does not have immortality within its flow of energy, but is weak and failing. A child with an ailment. A child who will not be immortal unless the entity acts.

When Simeon is calm and the room is quiet, perhaps when Marietta is having a snooze after lunch or watching afternoon TV Simeon thinks. If it is a bright day the sun shines right into the kitchen warming the oak furniture and creating shafts of light. In it he can see something, a denser shadow flitting through the air like fireflies darting and alive with energy. If he concentrates, the energy talks to him. It vibrates with a questioning hum. It is a very peaceful sensation.

Today, though, Simeon feels tired. It has been one of his school days when he's collected by the bus. The journey back has made him feel shaken and grumpy. All day demands have been asked of his body, which his body has not wanted to do. He has been pushed and pummelled. Instead of sitting strapped safely into his chair, he is put on the floor and he feels stranded. Every now and then his arm or leg will brush against something solid. His limbs are of no use to him, and he cannot tell anybody how uncomfortable he is. Even when he screams nothing comes to his aid. He is aware of other screams around him as if there is an echo. One event frustrates him more than the others. It is when he sees coloured lights flash on and off. He observes them and knows his response has some effect on their pattern, but he can't understand the meaning behind them. Surely there is a message? One he cannot fathom. Now Simeon is back at home, everything is calm again. He can smell the familiar smells and hear the expected hum around him. But then there is a sudden change in the atmosphere. Simeon is aware of it but does not know the reason.

Kate has come back. Marietta notices the change of mood too. She thinks Kate might have contracted a fever, her colour is heightened, her brow looks sweaty and her eyes too bright. And, unusually, her first words are not to ask about Simeon's morning.

'Oh, God, I hope Ambrose gets back soon.'

Marietta winces at the blasphemy but says nothing; instead she walks over to the sink to fill the kettle.

She wishes Kate would calm down; she is always fidgeting, which unsettles Simeon. She tries not to sigh as she asks, 'Did you want to tell me, Mrs Isherwood?'

Kate is not in the habit of confiding in Marietta. She knows she shouldn't be mentioning this to anybody anyway. But she can't help it. The secret is too big for her to carry on her own. Ignoring Marietta's frown, she turns to Simeon. 'Sweetheart,' she says, placing her hand on his, 'We might be able to make you better.'

She can tell him; after all, he is not going to pass the information on. And Marietta is at the sink. Even if she eavesdrops, she won't say anything either.

Marietta stops filling the kettle. She wonders if she has heard correctly or whether the noise of water has muffled the words. Her skin prickles as if the room has become loaded with alarm. What are they thinking of doing to Simeon? She is too overcome to say anything more than, 'What?'

Kate continues to speak to Simeon. 'Yes, they've said the gene replacement might go ahead. Isn't that fantastic?' Her smile is so bright that Simeon is aware of a wave of heat coming from her.

Marietta sees herself shrink in the reflection of the chrome kettle; warped. The idea is grotesque. When she prayed for God's help, she didn't think it would come in the guise of gene therapy. This is the recipe of the Devil. She shudders and feels forced to say something.

'Are you sure that's a good idea? It's like... it's like tampering with God's creation.'

Kate continues to ruffle Simeon's hair.

'Come and sit down,' Marietta says, concerned that Kate is going to upset Simeon by her fidgeting.

Kate steps over to the kitchen table and sits down resting her head in her hands.

Kate and Simeon both hear the noise of the kettle and the clatter of the cups and teapot being prepared. It is a familiar ritual, which calms them both.

'Here you are, Mrs Isherwood,' Marietta says, putting a cup of tea in front of Kate.

Kate doesn't have the energy for thanks, so says nothing. She puts sugar in her tea and stirs it, watching the circular motion of the liquid.

'Talking about it might help?' Marietta says, for once pulling out a chair and sitting down opposite Kate.

The whole concept is so vast that Kate doesn't think she would be able to put into words how she is feeling. The initial euphoria has faded. All she can see are obstacles, problems and loopholes.

Marietta continues, 'When I have a problem, I ask Jesus to help me.' When Kate says nothing she goes on, 'Yes, when it is very difficult I ask myself, *What would Jesus do?* and I pray.'

Kate's mouth opens but she does not speak. What she wants to say is, 'Well. Jesus would just wave his hand, wouldn't he, and make the dumb talk and the blind see and the crippled walk'. Kate turns in her seat and looks at Simeon in his isolation. He is smiling. Sometimes he laughs for no reason and other times he becomes so agitated that he works himself up into a fit. Simeon has a globule of drool running down his chin, about to drip onto his shirt; she should go over and wipe it but she can't make her body move. When Simeon smiles, Kate has no idea if it is because he is happy and contented, or if it is just part of his disorder. In the beginning they tried very hard to establish some method of communication but nothing worked. She wishes she knew his thoughts, it would make this easier.

She stirs her tea again and watches the cool, undrunk liquid move just as it did before.

Simeon is aware of the stillness in the room following the initial activity. Now there is a small chink, chink, chink noise, which he can perceive in the stillness, he likes its regular rhythm. He taps his finger to the sound, on his chair, but neither Kate nor Marietta notices.

'Do you want to say a prayer?' Marietta asks. Kate shakes her head. She wants to cry but her eyes remain dry.

Finally she chokes out the words, 'I just want him to be...' but she can't finish the sentence. After all, what does she want him to be? Another child... a different child...a normal child.

'There, there, Mrs Isherwood,' Marietta murmurs. She reaches over and pats Kate's hand. Kate does not pull away.

'Let me get you some more tea. Hot tea.'

The latch on the back door clicks open and Kate hears a familiar, 'Yoo Hoo! Anybody here?' It is her mother's usual greeting and it immediately annoys Kate because, if the door is on the latch, somebody is at home.

However, at her mother's voice she sits up straight and brushes her eyes with the back of her hand. She grins to ensure any indication of sadness is eradicated from her face before her mother enters.

Simeon hears the 'Yoo Hoo' sound. It makes a ringing in his head. He has heard it before, lots of times. His brain repeats the sound, 'Oo, oo, Oo oo.' He tilts his head from side to side so it rolls around. But he is unable to vocalise the sound. All he can achieve is, 'Mm, Mmm.'

'Oh, look he's pleased to see me,' Norma says, as she bounds into the kitchen. She is petite and blonde, with a youthful vigour and deportment that belie her age.

'Who's a good boy then?' She approaches Simeon and pats his cheek.

He doesn't like the sensation of the slap against his flesh and is about to scream, but the patting stops and he grins instead.

Norma has dribble on the edge of her hand. She takes a wet wipe from the box beside Simeon and wipes each finger with exaggerated force, while staring at Simeon's smiling face.

'His hair needs a cut,' she instructs and then, 'Cup of tea, Marietta, while you're up.'

She takes the chair opposite Kate. 'You look peaky, dear.'

Kate shrugs. 'Long day.'

Norma gives a little shake of her head as she says, 'Well, you knew what you'd taken on when you went back to work. I told you it would be hard.'

Kate remembers the conversation well, even though it has been about six years since the original discussion. The conversation had begun as soon as she had mentioned the idea of returning to work and continued for six months afterwards. One line that repeats in Kate's memory is, 'I hope you don't think I'm going to play nursemaid for that boy.'

'Is Ambrose still doing that inane celebrity TV show?'

Kate nods.

Marietta puts the refilled teapot and a cup for Norma between them on the table. Norma picks the cup up, scrutinising it for signs of poor cleaning before it is filled. Finding none, she replaces it on the saucer and waits for Kate to pour her tea.

'It's beneath him, a show like that. I wonder why he does it?'

While busy pouring tea, Kate finds she is finally able to speak.

'He said it was a good way of promoting science to a younger generation. To those who might not access it otherwise.'

'Ha. Promoting science, my foot. I think you've got blinkers on your eyes again, letting him cavort in that den of iniquity.'

'We discussed it. He wanted to go.'

Norma takes a sip of her tea.

'That's your trouble; you always give in to him. Always. Look at the poor boy.'

She turns and points at Simeon.

Kate isn't exactly sure how to answer her mother's argument but doesn't have the will to respond. A long time ago she learnt that the way Norma sees things is the right way, especially if you are her only child.

Something moves in Simeon's field of vision. A movement of a limb. He reciprocates the motion by lifting his own hand, but his control is poor, so it flails in the air.

'Would you like some tea, little one?' Marietta asks Simeon.

She picks up a plastic beaker with a lid and a spout and tries to fold Simeon's fingers around it.

The cup feels heavy in Simeon's hand but with Marietta's fingers still around his, his hand feels steadier. The warmth is pleasant on his skin. 'Mm, Mmm,' he says.

'M, M, M, Marietta, that's it,' Marietta says, smiling. Still steadying his grip, she helps him sip the tepid liquid.

She is unaware of the look Norma is giving her. 'I don't think he's trying to say your name Marietta.'

'Well, he is trying to say something,' is Marietta's retort.

Kate remains silent; this is an argument she wants to remain clear of.

'It's likely to be an innate response and means absolutely nothing.'

Kate wonders why Marietta continually has this exchange with Norma, considering that Marietta knows Norma has a linguistics degree and was a head teacher.

'Well, I think he is trying to say my name.'

# IV

Entities should not have problems. If they do, they should have the capability to solve them. But our entity does have a problem, and is contemplating an experiment to solve it.

Ambrose arrives home in the early afternoon. The taxi drops him at the end of the drive. He has had to put up with an inane one-sided conversation all the way from the airport. The driver was an avid Mallory fan.

'She's gorgeous.' Wolf whistle.

'Is she as gorgeous in the flesh?' Wink, wink. Look down at chest, one hand off the steering wheel to gesture large breasts. Wink, wink.

The fact is, Ambrose liked Mallory... She was straightforward. She said and got what she wanted. It was why she was such a commercial success. For a girl who liked to play the blonde bimbo, she was actually very smart. Ambrose would have liked to tell the taxi driver this, but didn't get the opportunity.

'You did alright for an old chap.' Although Ambrose was desperate to leave, he feels a contradictory pride in not having been in the first few voted off. There were no loved ones to welcome him as he left the jungle. But, instead of being upset, he felt only relief that Kate and Simeon weren't there. As if they belonged to some alternate universe.

'But you were never going to win, were you? It's going to be that Mallory girl. I'd put money on it.'

The journey lasts over thirty minutes and continues in the same vein the entire time. Occasionally Ambrose manages to give a monosyllabic answer.

'And did you really eat those insects?'

'Yes.'

'That's horrible. And those things as well? Never seen anybody manage that before.'

'Well...' Ambrose is about to explain, it all depends on how you look at things. You have to pretend you are not an Englishman but a tribal member who would naturally eat bugs and unusual body parts. But he doesn't get a chance.

'Man, that is quite a sick stunt. I don't believe you did it. It's just TV, innit?'

Even when he gets to the back door, Ambrose doesn't feel quite able to enter his house. He needs a moment to collect himself before speaking to Simeon and Marietta. He is glad Kate will still be at work. He unlatches the back door as quietly as he can; it still lets out a little creak. Once inside, he leans his back against the door and drops his bag beside him. He closes his eyes and inhales the familiar scents of home.

Simeon is aware of the creak. It usually precedes something but he cannot connect what. The house is silent again but he can sense a movement of air. Something is there, not the usual energy he detects but a warmer being entirely. He tries to listen harder, but he can only hear the pulse of the blood through his head, making a whooshing sound, making him dizzy.

Ambrose feels exhausted. He opens his eyes and sees the black and white tiles of the floor, they blur into a dazzle of shattered segments in front of him. The dusty air of the gunroom is soothing. There is no longer the smell of polish and resin he remembers from his childhood, nor the rows of shiny brogues and muddy boots from that time. Now there is only a pair of gardening shoes, Marietta's outdoor shoes and some Wellingtons. They are dust-covered not having been worn for some time. He closes his eyes again, shutting out the whole world, and inhales deeply. He had once imagined he would have at least four children and the gunroom would have rows of shoes and boots of different sizes and colours, perhaps footballs and tennis rackets and jumbles of coats on the racks. He can visualise it so clearly that he wonders whether somewhere this parallel universe exists. If he opened his eyes now, could he be transported there?

Almost instinctively, he pushes a pair of shoes aside and sits down on the long wooden bench underneath the coat rack. It wobbles under his weight. He is reminded of hiding here as a child. Then he was small enough to squeeze into the corner. He was invisible under the fall of his father's heavy wool coat when he should have been in bed, but even in his pyjamas he was warm in his hiding place. From here he could listen to muted adult conversations drifting through from the lounge. Eavesdropping was exciting, although he sometimes couldn't understand the words. He'd hear the clink of the decanter and glasses and know important things were being discussed.

One of Kate's old jackets hangs from a peg. It is red. He can't remember her ever wearing it. It looks too vibrant, as if her body could never inhabit the folds of fabric. A scarf hangs beside it. It smells of her perfume; jasmine with an undertone of something spicy. He has missed her but doesn't know whether he wants to see her just yet. Sometimes the thought of her is better than the reality.

When they are apart he remembers someone carefree, laughing. Now she has dark shadows beneath her eyes and instead of the upright posture she'd had, she hunches her shoulders as if burdened down. They often went walking for miles across the Yorkshire moors and dales. He would tell her the geological history of every outcrop and valley, about how the earth had folded and been bent into shape over millennia. She would listen patiently, though she had heard it many times before. Now instead of accompanying him on walks she rarely wants to go further than the garden.

With a final sigh, Ambrose manages to move. He walks to the kitchen door and looks in to see Marietta frowning over a newspaper puzzle and Simeon grinning, his head twisting around as if he is following the movement of a fly flitting about the room.

'Hello,' he says.

Marietta almost jumps out of her chair and drops her pen. 'Oh, you shocked me, Mr Isherwood.'

Simeon registers the word, 'Hell-o.' It is a nice sound, an up-and-down sound. He grins and moves his arms as well as his head, as if conducting the syllables.

Marietta has gained her composure. 'How was your trip, Mr Isherwood? We loved watching you on the television.' She turns to include Simeon, 'Didn't we, little man?'

Simeon can't respond but knows something is happening around him. He kicks his feet as well as moving his hands and head. His grin gets wider and he manages to murmur, 'Mmm.'

Ambrose says, 'Well, it was an experience, let's just say that.'

He goes over to Simeon and picks up a wipe to clean the drool from his mouth.

'So Simeon, have you been behaving while I've been away?'

'He's been fine, Mr Isherwood. Just the same,' Marietta answers. 'I expect you'd like a proper cup of English tea.'

Ambrose simply nods his head. 'That would be nice, thank you Marietta.'

Marietta smiles as she puts the kettle on. She is glad Mr Isherwood is home. He is so polite and much more relaxed than Mrs Isherwood. She considers telling him about the possible treatment for Simeon but then thinks better of it. She has to leave that up to Mrs Isherwood and God of course. Perhaps He will intervene to stop the mad idea. It's what she has been praying for. And she is confident Mr Isherwood will do the right thing as well.

# V

The entity exists without fear of predators. If things were as they should be, it could meander through this universe and those that lie beyond. But things are not what they should be. There is the child. The child is the entity's purpose.

As Kate comes in from her day at work, she notices Ambrose's shoes in the gun room. The relief that he is here makes her light-headed, so she has to put her hand on the wall to steady herself. Thank goodness he is home.

She goes into the kitchen and smiles at Simeon, who grins blindly back at her.

Marietta is ironing when Kate enters. She doesn't look up but continues to sweep the iron over a skirt. 'Mr Isherwood is home.'

'Yes, I noticed his shoes,' Kate says.

'He's in his study.'

Kate prepares her own mug of tea and then heads up the stairs. She hesitates at the turn in the landing, where a step down leads to the door of Ambrose's study. She contemplates knocking. But she can't think what she wants to say. It is enough that he is home. She continues up a few more steps, her tea slopping onto the carpet, leaving a trail of brown circles.

The light is gloomy in the master bedroom, which faces northwards over the front drive. Kate sits at her dressing table for a long time looking at her three reflections in the triptych mirror. It is odd to be split into three images. Perhaps each doppelgänger has a different existence. One might be single and involved in cutting-edge research, with a list of letters after her name, another might be the doting mother of a boy and girl destined for fame, and the third might be married and divorced and beginning an exciting new life as a singleton. The triplets look back at her unblinking, wondering who Kate is, how her life differs from theirs.

Ambrose is sitting at his desk. It is a wide, heavy piece of furniture, passed down through generations of Isherwoods. He strokes the wood, allowing his finger to trace the familiar knots and grain. Hearing a creak on the stairs his back stiffens, and then relaxes as the footsteps move on.

His view from this window is superb. From here he can see the hills in the distance. The outline of those hills is so familiar to him. He has researched them as one might trace an ancestral line. He has divined their individual traits and characteristics. Ambrose senses they are part of his history. As if they have been there forever, linking the past to the present.

Darker clouds are gathering over the peaks and creating patches of shadow as they move over the fields between the house and hills. Behind the garden is a paddock, where there is meant to be a horse, but where in fact there is simply long grass and wild flowers. At the end of the garden are trees, amidst them a copper beech, Ambrose's favourite.

Once there was a pond where, as a child, Ambrose used to play and fish. He remembers spending a whole day watching tadpoles break out from their individual sacs and start to swim. He must have been about six. He had lain on his stomach and watched. He recalls the sun changing position in the sky as the spawn below him gradually changed from a dotted jelly to a moving black mass. Nobody had disturbed him. He hadn't even returned to the house for a drink or lunch. Perhaps a year later he had told his mother about this day. She had said, 'No, Ambrose. We would never have let you play by the pond unsupervised.' His father was also dismissive, 'It takes longer than a day for tadpoles to hatch. I think you must have imagined it.' But Ambrose was sure of what he'd seen. After that he was reluctant to share his ideas with his parents for fear of being labelled a liar. Anyway there were no tadpoles now. No pond. When Simeon was born they thought it best to get rid of it, thinking he'd walk and be capable of accidents.

From a distance, Ambrose hears a faint 'Yoo Hoo,' and, from the hall, echoing up the stairs, 'Katherine, are you there?' He hears steps on the staircase. *'Fi, Fo, Fi, Fum'*. It is a whisper in his brain, unbidden. He gets up from his desk and goes towards the door. He moves silently. Breathing quietly, as he has been taught when tracking a wild animal. He hides behind his door.

Then Norma is outside his room. 'Katherine... Katherine... Katherine.' The voice gets louder with each call.

Ambrose wonders whether to go out, but is grateful when he hears Kate's reply. 'Just coming Mum. I'll be down in a minute.'

'Don't be long. Marietta wants to go home.'

Ambrose can sense Norma outside his door, waiting for Kate to say something else, but when nothing more is forthcoming, he finally hears her footsteps receding as she returns to the kitchen.

A few minutes later he hears Kate pass his doorway. Then he goes back to his desk and his view.

'So Ambrose is back,' is Norma's greeting as Kate enters the kitchen.

Marietta is ready to leave, with her basket in hand and her coat on. She shuffles out like some scurrying creature with a fleeting, 'Good bye.'

'So what are you having for Ambrose's homecoming dinner?' Norma asks.

Kate hasn't thought about food for some time. Her brain has been taken over by the prospect of Simeon's treatment and how she will tell Ambrose.

'I don't know.'

'How can you not know what you're eating for supper? Don't you ever use the planner I gave you?'

'I don't always have time to cook. There's probably a microwave meal in the freezer.' Kate ambles over to the kitchen sink, from where she can look down the garden. The sky is getting darker. The wind is rising; the leaves of the copper beech are ripples of dark brown edged with gold. Belatedly she asks Norma, 'Do you want to stay for dinner?'

'I don't think so. I think it better if I go and leave you to look after your husband and child.' Kate hasn't even turned around to say 'goodbye' before she hears the back door close. If she didn't know her mother better, she might have called it a slam. But it must have been the wind.

Simeon hears the bang of the door and laughs. He lifts each foot and lets it drop, *bang, bang, bang* against his chair.

'Simeon, what are you doing?' Kate asks.

Ambrose appears in the doorway. Although he has lost a little weight, he looks too large to come through it. Kate wants to run towards him, fling herself at his bulk and feel that old scratchy jumper rub against her cheek. But she doesn't have the energy to run. She has a headache beginning. It's just a faint throbbing in her right temple. It must be the impending storm and Simeon's steady kicking. She turns back to the window. Clouds are surging across the sky, saturated with imminent rain, turning darker and more turbulent as she watches. The wind is whipping the branches of the beech tree, they flail in frenzy. The leaves twist between black and purple, a movement, which reminds her of congealing blood.

Ambrose waits in the doorway, hesitating. Simeon looks agitated; he is banging his feet up and down. The light through the window, strobing from dark to brightness under the storm clouds, gives everything a strange glow. He imagines ions loading and unloading their charge in an orgy overhead. When Kate finally turns to face him again, her face is flushed and her eyes too bright.

'Guess what's happened,' she says. The words seem to sputter from her lips like a mouthful of too-hot tea. She had no idea she was going to blurt it out.

In the doorway Ambrose looks stricken. What crisis has occurred now? Surely she can't be pregnant. Or perhaps she is having a breakdown. He has suspected that Kate might have bipolar disorder; occasionally she has had bouts of severe depression, which swing to a state of euphoria.

'Don't look so shocked,' she says, smiling at him, 'And don't worry, it's good news.' Kate isn't at all sure it is good news, but the sight of Ambrose's features had taken on a look of such distress she feels forced to say something.

'How was your trip, though? It looked exciting.'

Ambrose breathes out. This is the conversation he was expecting.

'To be truthful, it was pretty awful. They call it 'reality' television, but it's the least real place I have ever been to. The set is artificial, the conversations...everything is contrived.'

Finally Ambrose comes into the kitchen and sits at the table.

'Simeon, please stop kicking.' He reaches over and puts a hand on one of Simeon's legs.

Simeon feels the hand against his limb. It is warm and heavy.

'It was a total waste of time. I learned nothing and those celebrities will have insects dropped on them and crawl through mud; but ask to prick their finger for a drop of blood or put an electrode on their skin and they suddenly become squeamish! I was a fool to accept the invitation.'

Ambrose continues, 'Now, what about your news? You said you had something to tell me.'

Kate watches Ambrose; his hand remains on Simeon's leg. Simeon's leg is so spindly the hand looks massive. She can see the freckles and the hairs sticking out, as if they've been magnified. Even though Simeon has stopped kicking, her headache is getting worse. She is having difficulty distinguishing the pumping of her heart from the rolling thunder outside. Kate's mouth has become dry. She gets a glass from the cupboard and fills it with water. Her hands are wet on the glass as she gulps it down.

'Simeon, they think...' She has to stop, the words are jumbling in her mouth, her tongue feels swollen with the shock of what she is about to say, 'Kamir thinks...' She coughs and takes another sip of water... Taking a breath she tries again.

'...Kamir Mehta thinks they might be ready to do an op on Simeon. Genetic replacement.'

Pattering raindrops strike the window pane. Simeon begins to hum in response to the vibration they make.

'That is... that's...' But what is it? For once, Ambrose has no words; no sound comes out of his mouth. Is it incredible, or is it dangerous? Is it even possible?

Ambrose senses Simeon's kicking has stopped, but he keeps his hand there. He wishes he could communicate with Simeon. Now, with his hand against Simeon's leg, there is a sense of interaction, some deeper bond. He wants to find a link, something that will unlock Simeon. Something that could reveal his son.

Perhaps Kamir Mehta's idea is what they have been waiting for. Suddenly Ambrose is out of his chair. He hugs Kate. She is startled by this sudden intimacy. A giggle catches in her throat at the pleasant swirling sensation in her stomach. Her head is still throbbing and she feels dizzy, but she lets Ambrose embrace her.

Simeon looks on, noticing the movement, and says, 'Mmm.'

# VI

The entity is present everywhere. Sometimes, humans try to reach a place of mind where they believe they communicate with it, feel some emotion or cause a reaction. A prayer, a spell, a wish. All mean nought to the entity. It remains unfathomable.

Marietta is lighting a candle in the church this morning. She does not worry that she might be late for work. This is far too important to rush. Every day for the past week, she has carried out this task, ever since Mrs Isherwood mentioned the awful plan. As the flame ignites she prays. She is reassured by the flickering burst of light that God is listening and breathing life to allow the flame to burn.

It is raining as she leaves the church and she puts up her umbrella. She still doesn't hurry up the hill though but walks along the east end of the churchyard. She stops at a simple stone cross carved from pinkish granite. It marks the resting place of Alfred Homerton; Born Oct 1820. Died Dec 1882. Marietta has no connection to him or his family. She does not know if he was an important man or not. But Marietta likes the monument because of the inscription 'In his light shall we see light'. She thinks of the little candle flame flickering on in the darkness of the church and repeats her prayer. As she waits, she realises the fall of raindrops onto the umbrella has stopped and weak sunlight is trying to break through. She takes it as a sign, and crosses herself.

She is pleased it is a Monday. Simeon will be picked up by the bus to take him to school; in fact, a specialist centre. While he's there, she has the house to herself and time to think as she cleans and tidies. As she turns in at the gravelled drive she admires the grey brick Victorian building. She is not envious, for that would be a sin, but she does occasionally wish she owned a house like it. Sometimes, she imagines that she is the owner, perhaps married to a man like Ambrose. Not Ambrose, of course, because to contemplate that would be sinful. Her own home is a modest terrace house on the outskirts of the city. It has enough room for her and her few belongings, and space for her daughter's occasional visits. But it hasn't got much of a garden and the rooms are rather small and gloomy.

'If I owned this house,' she thinks, 'I would use the front door.' The back door has been modified with a ramp to make it easier for Simeon's wheelchair, so that has become the main entrance. As Marietta passes the porch, with its stained glass panes and triangles of bright tiling, she notices a few leaves long left from the autumn. They have almost disintegrated to brown dust and are caught up with cobwebs. Although it is not part of her job to clean outside the house, she makes a point to clear them out today. It is not a good or welcoming thing to have an abandoned front door.

As she approaches the back door she can hear Simeon's high-pitched scream.

Kate had a message from Kamir Mehta this morning. A three word email that makes her nauseous. 'Any decision yet?' Kamir's deadline is approaching; she and Ambrose need to talk. She phones Marietta.

The phone call is like some early warning signal to Marietta. Her hand trembles as Kate asks her to prepare a meal for this evening. Marietta can tell by the way Kate asks that this is not a fancy romantic gesture. This is a summit.

When Kate returns home, Marietta instructs her that the lasagne will just need reheating and clingfilm cover removing from the salad. Kate notes the clipped tones, which shoot at her like spittle. Marietta won't look at her. Instead, she clatters the pans as she dries up. 'So is this a special occasion, Mrs Isherwood?'

'No, not really,' Kate hesitates. Perhaps it is. It is certainly an occasion. An important one. 'I just have something to discuss with Ambrose. It's always easier with a nice meal and a glass of wine.'

She regards Marietta's back hunched over the sink and wonders why a wave of guilt sweeps over her. She shouldn't have to explain herself to Marietta. 'Anyway, thank you.'

'You are welcome, Mrs Isherwood,' Marietta responds to the pan in her hand, watching her reflection's distorted mouth saying the words.

For once, Simeon has settled quickly. Marietta is long gone and Kate is waiting for Ambrose to return. The comfortable smell of lasagne is diffusing through the house. The grandfather clock chimes eight o'clock, the sound swelling and then fading from the hall to the kitchen. When it has stopped the house seems too quiet, as if it is holding its breath. Waiting.

In Limbo. Kate feels that is her permanent state at present. Awaiting a point that may never arrive. She checks her pulse, pressing two fingers against her wrist. The blood is moving at a steady pace. Blood that is always in motion. A substance that does not pause. A pause would be disastrous.

Where the hell is Ambrose? Why does he have to be late tonight? She pours herself some wine. It clings to the balloon of the glass as she rotates it, emulating the distant range of purple hills. Kate has to refocus on the hills as they seem to be closer, as if they are creeping round the house to attend the meeting, to eavesdrop on the discussion, a force of centrifuge, pulling inwards. They are not malicious, just curious. Kate always thinks of them as Ambrose's hills. He used to tell her how each layer, every fold, every valley was created, as if he had been there at the beginning, an architect involved in the precise planning.

The back door slams.

'Mm, something smells good,' says Ambrose. Kate turns quickly and realises she should have checked the lasagne. The odour has changed from one of warmth to singeing.

'I'll just go and freshen up,' Ambrose says, and leaves the kitchen.

Kate hears the clock strike nine as Ambrose finally comes into the kitchen. He smiles and sits at the table. Slowly, Kate ladles lasagne onto their plates, aware of the blackened edges, aware that her hand is shaking. She watches as Ambrose puts forkfuls of food into his mouth. He does not comment on the dish. Kate takes a mouthful of the food. It is not very nice. She knows she needs to raise the matter of Simeon's operation but can't form the sentences she intended to say. Now the planned words seem to be congealing on her tongue like the burnt lasagne.

Her fork rings against the china plate. She takes a gulp of wine. Ambrose has nearly finished his meal.

'Not hungry?' he asks, looking at her and smiling, 'Bit crisp around the edges.'

Kate looks at him. It is time to talk. She opens her lips but it takes too long for the words to form in her mouth. Before she can speak, Ambrose has interrupted with, 'Sorry I was so late back. Lots of things to sort out.'

In fact, he is not that sorry he was late. It is just that Kate has been looking at him with such a frown of disapproval he needed to say something. The delay had been due to arrangements being made for Mallory to visit the research station. A surge of excitement makes him grin. He wonders if Kate will notice.

Finally, Kate manages to stutter out a sentence. 'I had a message from Kamir today. He wants to know what we've decided.'

Ambrose is still, like the hovering hawk preparing to strike, the merest tremble suggesting he will dive. Whilst Kate awaits his reply, she thinks she can hear the ticking of the hall clock. Each second drags, like drips of water quivering on the rim of a tap. The sudden loudness of Ambrose speaking in the silence makes Kate jump.

'I think we've got to do it,' he says. He realises he is shouting his words, as if the gradual build up to this decision has finally discharged.

Kate winces as if he has sworn at her with a torrent of expletives. She is surprised he seems so certain. She wishes she could speak with the same conviction.

'You seem sure.'

'I am now. What else can we do? I think we have to take the risk.'

Kate cannot answer, she feels sick, the small amount of lasagne she has eaten rolling like boulders in her stomach.

'Kate, Simeon's been given an opportunity. I think we have to take it.'

Kate makes a little noise in response; it should be a word but it tangles on her tongue.

'What would be worse than his present state?' Kate remains silent so Ambrose answers for her, 'Only death.'

The word is so large it seems to fill the room. Kate thinks it sounds like the grandfather clock striking one, resonating through the house, making every particle vibrate, reminding her that it is bricks and mortar and capable of collapse. When her breathing has steadied she manages to respond.

'I don't want him to die.'

'Neither do I, but the other possibility is that he lives. He has a life. A fuller life than he does now.'

Kate remains silent, pondering a life without Simeon. It gives her a physical pain in the centre of her being. She thinks of the grandfather clock again; how it annoys her at times with the imagined menace of 'Coming to find you!' when she has yet to decide on a place to hide. But the absence of sound, if the pendulum should stop swinging, would be with her all the time rather than each hour. She would miss it.

'Yoo Hoo, Anybody at home?'

'What the hell,' mutters Ambrose. 'What the hell is your mother doing here at this time of night?' He hisses the question across the table.

'I don't know,' Kate says, bristling at his accusation. She is asking herself the same question. Usually, she would have heard the car, or the click of the outer door.

'Well this looks cosy,' Norma says, as she enters the kitchen. 'I hope I didn't disturb you dropping in like this, but I needed to talk to you about your birthday, Katherine.'

Kate wonders how her mother can fail to realise the disruption she has caused. It feels so palpable, she expects to see visible ripples in the air.

'It's rather late for you to be visiting, Norma.'

'I know, Ambrose, but I was passing on my way back from choir practice.'

Kate mentally maps the route from the rehearsal room to the house and knows Norma is lying. It is out of her way. She won't mention this.

'It's a bit late to be eating a heavy meal. It'll go straight to your hips, Katherine.'

Kate's skirt feels as if it is tightening against her abdomen. She is half standing, half sitting, uncomfortable. She stands up and smoothes the material.

'What do you want, Mother?' Kate asks in a tired voice.

'Well, a coffee would be nice.'

Kate walks to fill the kettle, grateful for the plashing rush of water, which covers the sounds of her exasperation. She imagines her irritation zigging and zagging about her head in comic strip symbols.

In the background she can hear Ambrose moving the dishes to the dishwasher, a chore he rarely does, and Norma's voice having a one-sided conversation about the things that have filled her day.

Kate makes coffee in mugs and hopes her mother doesn't complain. Ambrose remains at the window looking out at the darkness. When Kate joins Norma at the table, Norma says, 'Now Katherine, have you thought about your birthday celebration?'

'I don't want to do anything.'

'But it's your fiftieth. You've got to have a party. It's a milestone.'

Kate imagines a row of white posts, way-markers edging a long road like gravestones counting down the descent to a dusty death. Is the purpose of anniversaries simply to mark out time, the inevitable countdown to oblivion?

The ancients used to acknowledge their important dates with the movement of the sun and moon and the flow of the tides. Without a calendar she would never remember important events. Soon she will be writing the date of Simeon's operation in her diary. Kate wonders what that event might portend, whether there will be an alteration in the orbit of the planet or the creation of a star.

'Katherine! Are you listening to me?'

Kate has to fight her way back from Space, where her thoughts have drifted.

'How about if I take you out for meal and a show?'

Kate does not want to go to a show with Norma. 'I can't concentrate on my birthday at the moment.' She has avoided telling Norma about Simeon's possible surgery, but Norma appears to know instinctively.

'Well, you should. That boy shouldn't be the only one considered in this family. You need some 'You' time.'

Norma reaches over and pats Kate's wrist. Kate knows she should be grateful but she can't raise the necessary emotion.

Kate wants to say something about the importance of this moment. It overrides every other decision she has ever made. It overshadows birthdays, anniversaries, wars and even moon landings. But she will not be able to explain this to Norma. It is not what Norma wants to hear.

'There're some good shows on at present. We could go to the West End. Or how about a theatre trip to Stratford? You can't beat the Royal Shakespeare Company.'

Kate shakes her head.

Norma tuts and says, 'Dear oh dear, you are in a state about something. Have you two been arguing?' She looks smug as if she has discovered their secret. 'Well, I'll leave you the theatre brochure,' Norma takes a booklet from her bag and places it on the table. 'You can have a look and let me know when you've decided.' Norma looks at her wristwatch. 'Now must dash. Busy, you know.' She shrugs in a charade of flightiness, but Kate knows her mother is organised to the point of OCD and that everything is under complete control.

She remains stationary while Norma kisses her cheek; the lips are warm and dry. The texture reminds her of a snake she once handled at a petting zoo.

When she hears the click of the back door latch at Norma's departure, she realises Ambrose has left the room.

# VII

We are all matter. Stuff of darkness, stuff of light. A watery soup of interactions creating a person. Held together by bonds, a woven network linking us to others, sharing thoughts and feelings. And at our core a link to the stars and space. And if we had the chance to make a difference, to heal a child, our own offspring, the likelihood is that we would take it. The entity is no different.

They have said 'Yes!' to Simeon's operation. 'Yes!' with an exclamation mark. At least, that is how Kate thinks of it every time she does think of it, which is often. She smiles at the orgasmic quality of its effect on her. Since the decision something appears to have changed. Here they are again, lazing in bed on a Saturday morning, having just made love. Their love-making has become frequent and vociferous, she repeating 'Yes!' and Ambrose vocalising a series of 'Mmms' of pleasure. It is strange as it is something she doesn't remember ever happening before.

Somewhere in her brain she senses the weight of the planning and operation looming ahead. But she fends the thought away for the present. Instead she luxuriates in Ambrose's arms and the sensation of owning a secret. It feels a little like the early days of her pregnancy, when only she knew for certain that the process had begun. Only her body was privy to the extraordinary multiplication of cells unfolding. Yes, that is exactly how it is. Simeon will be born again. New and complete. She snuggles further into Ambrose's shoulder and sighs.

Ambrose is laying against the pillows, his arm around Kate. Sometimes she seems very small. And since their decision she seems lighter, as if the burden that was weighing her down has been lifted. He hopes this mood will continue. The sex has also been a bonus. He had become resigned to the infrequency of the acts between them, but now they appear to be discovering each other all over again.

Kate moves her head against his shoulder and sighs, as if she knows she should start moving.

Ambrose strokes her hair and tries not to feel guilty. Ambrose has a secret. It is not the keeping of secrets which concerns him. He has kept many and makes sure that only information he is willing to share is passed on. But this is definitely a guilty secret. His skin beneath Kate's hair prickles with the idea of it and is not an unpleasant sensation. He knows he should feel ashamed.

As if reading his thoughts Kate asks, 'You know when you were in the jungle, did you talk to anybody much?'

Ambrose's response is a lie, this time his whole body prickles. 'No, not really, the cameras are on you most of the time so you have to be careful.' Indeed, he thinks, you did have to be very careful. But if you were clever you could evade the spies and occasionally have a heart to heart.

Again with worrying perceptiveness, Kate asks, 'What was Mallory like?'

'She was nice.' Ambrose is aware of the inadequacy of the words. He won't tell Kate about the night he managed to have a conversation with Mallory. They sat beside the campfire and watched the embers change from gold to amber through a spectrum of colours that he could have explained to her scientifically but didn't. Instead they talked about their lives, their dreams. He had to concentrate on the fire so he could conceal the physical desire he felt for her. The way the firelight glowed over her exposed skin, the way it changed the planes of her face and the movement of her mouth. Made him wonder about the nature of beauty. He was lucky to have seen so many spectacular and wonderful vistas in his time but the vision of a beautiful woman would always remain an enigma. As they talked, he'd realised Mallory was funny and humble, completely different to the persona she paraded for the TV and tabloids. Something about her had reminded him of a young Kate. Not in their appearance but in the way they saw the world, as if both had a secret knowledge that they might share with him.

'I like the name Mallory,' Kate says. 'Is it her real name or a pseudonym?'

'I don't know.' Ambrose is surprised that Mallory is the kind of name that appeals to Kate. When they were thinking about girls names before Simeon was born she had always suggested traditional names. But she was right; Mallory was a good, strong name. 'I didn't think you liked unusual names.'

'Well, maybe not for my own daughter.'

Ambrose would have liked a daughter. A child with the name Elizabeth or Rebecca. He imagines a bright and pretty child who appeared to make the world a better place. Yes, he would have loved to have had a daughter.

Ambrose strokes Kate's hair again and lets his hand travel over her shoulder onto her breast. It feels soft but has lost the tautness it once had. Now Mallory's name has been mentioned, he can't help comparing her firm breasts and her skin, an alluring temptation in the flickering flame, with Kate's pale, slack flesh. Each time they have made love since his return he has been unable to keep the image of Mallory out of his mind. He has imagined that toned body beneath his hands as an exquisite discovery and has difficulty in refraining from shouting 'Mallory!' as he comes. Thankfully, up until now he has managed to hold back to a moan of 'Mmm, Mmm, Mmm.' He is not sure to whom he is being most disloyal.

# VIII

Like gravity, the entity is always present, in every action, every reaction. The entity exists in the spaces between atoms and in the vast emptiness between stars; it influences everything and knows what happens next, though we do not appreciate its prescience.

Kate is sewing. The jab of the needle pierces the fabric trailing a flare of red thread. Under the parasol, she is in her own circle of shade, she has her sewing box beside her. It has been so long since she'd looked at it, all the yarn had tangled together while neglected. Patiently she has undone them. The embroidered scene is half a summer's garden. She pulls the scarlet yarn through the material. It will make a rose. Each movement of her hand is constructing this segment of her universe. A violet thread becomes a lavender flower, green a leaf; piece-by-piece she is the source of the creation. The noises remind her of a pulse; 'phtt' and 'psst' as the needle stabs and guides the thread.

She pauses in her stitching for a moment, watches Ambrose's figure bending over the flowerbed. The hoe turns the earth with a similar swish and twist rhythm. He is weeding, something he rarely does but this is a strange afternoon. They are all out in the garden. Kate cannot remember the last time they were all together like this in restful companionship.

It has been such a warm day that there is a haze below the line of hills, smudging the heather into bruises. The breeze rises and falls with its own irregular rhythm, so at moments the rustling of the copper beech canopy becomes a rattle, and then is silent. In the quiet phases she can hear the sound of the thread below her fingers; a gentle ripping. The garden sounds create a muted symphony, the movement of leaves, the buzz of a bee, the occasional bleat of a sheep and the scrape of the hoe over dry soil. There is also a different humming, more human. It takes a moment for her to realise the noise is emanating from her. She is humming a tune. Greensleeves. She smiles and hums a little louder. The summer sun is warm on her skin. It glints with green reflections off the chrome of Simeon's wheelchair, making him blend with the scenery. For once he is quiet, with only the occasional gurgle or flailing of a limb.

Simeon sits in his chair under the copper beech. On his head is a floppy straw hat. It creates square freckles on his face. When he looks up he sees the spiky fringe where the hat has frayed. Beyond that is the leaf canopy of the tree reaching up to the sky. Simeon is unaware of where the hat ends and the tree trunk begins. He has no comprehension of the trunk giving way to branches, to twigs and finally to leaves, because the leaves bleed into the sky without boundary. The foliage is just beginning to change from copper to brown, heralding the end of summer, but Simeon knows nothing of the changing seasons. A leaf is released from the tree and floats slowly to the ground, in a motion, which suggests that it could be held in the palm of a hand, tenderly protecting its fall.

Kate watches Ambrose bend and stretch; he has a weed in his gloved hand and tosses it backwards onto a small pile behind him. He stops often, as if he is watching something, the flight of a butterfly or a ladybird scuttling along a twig, a beetle crawling in the undergrowth. There is no need for him to undertake this chore anyway, they have a gardener who comes in three times a week. Kate has become drowsy, her needle becoming slower. She watches Ambrose's arms bend and flex, the same arms that embraced her that morning. She watches the pull as his neck muscles tighten when he bends and remembers kissing the stubble between his ear and jaw. She admires the swell of his calf muscle as it stretches and contracts, thinking of her toes pressed against his legs as she moved below him that morning. She closes her eyes and sighs, marvelling at the power of lovemaking to create such a feeling of comfort in her. She knows it is simply endorphins triggered in her brain, but it doesn't matter. That power seems stronger than any other. An addictive drug.

She glances at the oriental poppies in the border, huge pinky-purple petals like folds of skin layered into ruffles, sees the ripe testicular pods ready to burst with new blooms. She licks her lips. Since the decision to proceed with Simeon's operation, their lovemaking has been almost daily and more vigorous than ever before. She opens her eyes again and watches his buttocks stretch the fabric of his shorts and feels a warm anticipation between her legs.

Simeon's head is full of sound. It changes in intensity and cadence. Long whistles, vibrations and sing-song voices that ebb and flow and bubble. With flecks of light dancing over his eyelids and the sensations in his ears, he has an orchestra in his control. He starts to dip and tilt his head so the notes swirl around and he tries to lift his limbs to the rhythm. His hat has tipped back so his face is exposed. High up a butterfly passes creating a shadow over Simeon's upturned face. The absence of photons empties the silhouette of substance so he senses the shadow like kisses touching his skin. It tickles. He laughs.

Ambrose is watching a bee crawling over a flower. Its fat, black and yellow body is dusty, wearing bloomers of pollen. It lifts from the flower, hums above the lavender, manoeuvring before landing on the next blossom.

'Can you hear that, Simeon?'

He notices Simeon's hat is askew and goes over to pull it down so Simeon's skin is protected again. Simeon is aware of Ambrose's shadow. There is a marked change in illumination. But now it feels comfortable. He is not afraid...

Ambrose knows it does not matter if Simeon can hear the insect or not, but he wants to share a thought, a detail about nature, with his son.

'*Bombus terrestris*, that's the biological name for this Bumble Bee. *Bombus terrestris*. Lovely, don't you think? My Uncle Rex told me all the names of the insects and plants. He was the one who made me interested in natural sciences.'

In Simeon's orchestra a new beat has been added. He hears the weight of the words bouncing against his eardrum. *Bom, Bom, Bombus*. His hand swings and knocks into his chair in time.

'Once upon a time, they thought bumble bee flight should be impossible,' Ambrose scrutinises Simeon's face for the merest hint of understanding, finding none he continues, 'Its wings seem too small for its big body to give it enough lift.' Ambrose points at the creature crawling over the lavender. 'But even though its wings work independently of each other and aerodynamically it's a mess, it still manages to do what needs to be done. Brilliant isn't it?' Ambrose laughs, delighted to be vocalising the joy he has at the marvels of nature. Simeon laughs in reciprocation and waves his arms about. The sunlight is creating shadows to move across his face when the leaves ripple. Kate smiles as Ambrose talks to Simeon. She grins at the normality of the afternoon. Stitching, weeding and sitting.

The scent of lavender suffuses the air making her drowsy, her needlework has almost stopped but she breathes deeply, enjoying the sensation of being filled with fragrant air. Then, somewhere from the distant hedgerow Kate hears a bird calling. It has gradually become louder and is now a persistent cry she cannot ignore. She wonders if a fledging has got lost amidst the border of bushes. She can't work out if it is the mother or the chick making the distressing call. She remembers that at some point they are going to have to discuss the details of Simeon's operation. Though the smooth comfort of the afternoon softens the thought, she knows that soon the harsh reality of the procedure is going to take over. Like a normal pregnancy, the undesirable realisation that the process of giving birth has to be overcome. The wrenching of a new body from an old one cannot be avoided. She shudders even though it is not cold. Her needle stutters and pierces her thumb, letting a drop of blood stain the fabric. Her embroidery garden gains a real bloody rose.

'*Bom, Bom, Bom,*' the rhythm repeats in Simeon's head. His hand striking against his chair intensifies so a new '*Bang, Clang, Bang,*' metallic sound is added. The cacophony whirls around and within him.

Kate looks over anxiously; she is sucking her thumb to stem the bleeding. From stillness and peace she is aware that Simeon has become animated.

'Do you think Simeon's alright?' she calls to Ambrose.

Ambrose stands, stretching his back, and looks towards Simeon. After a couple of seconds of perusal he answers, 'Yes, I think so. Perhaps he just needs to be moved, he's been sitting still for a while.'

Ambrose moves to Simeon and pushes the chair a short distance so he is looking back at the house rather than towards the beech tree. Then he lifts up each of Simeon's legs and massages them and reclines the chair a little to adjust the pressure on Simeon's body. He has the sudden image of what life will be like after Simeon's operation, when there will be no need to move chairs or massage legs. A day when Simeon will be able to race down the garden, whooping and shouting. Instead of massaging the twig-like limbs, one day he'll be able to lift Simeon's leg up into a stirrup and feel the weight of the boy in his hands as he helps him mount a pony. The faint whinny of a horse bubbles on the breeze and Ambrose turns his head to the paddock, certain he should see the form of a pony, which, one day, will exist.

Simeon's limbs feel light as his father moves them. A weightlessness held by a stronger force. He senses the support of the chair beneath his body and knows that without the straps on the chair his body would be capable of flight. He laughs.

# IX

The entity has a plan... It is not a plan as a human would interpret it. No flow chart. No little boxes with input arrows, chugging diligently to an output... *Plop*... At the other end... The entity is without beginning and ending. Its plan is but a wave of energy spilling into a greater universe not yet fully formed. This universe will only exist when humans begin to recognise it and give it a name, as if it is their invention rather than something beyond their imagination. The entity though, has no comprehension or concern about anything other than its offspring.

Kate is unable to sleep, her mind is a hub leading to the one central thought. What will happen? She can hear the wind blowing, building towards a storm. It sounds like a creature circling the house, moving faster and faster, until it blurs into a mirage, speeding around the house, an obstacle in its path. How it can be so wild, she wonders. After all it is only air moving from one place to another. Sometimes, the wind sounds as if it is the aggressor, bashing things, tossing everything around, but tonight it sounds like a victim, as if it is being dragged reluctantly across the earth, gripping trees and gables and steeples, holding onto the house with fingernails screeching.

Finally, Kate gets up. The nightlight on the landing gives out a diffuse glow, leaching the colour from objects, making everything insubstantial. She descends the stairs and heads to Simeon's room at the front of the house. At the doorway she pauses, he appears to be sleeping deeply. He is so still, she has to go into the room and reassure herself that he is breathing. He is curled beneath his bedclothes; the shape reminds her of a shell. The nightlight emits a yellow bloom, illuminating the rise and fall of the duvet. She has the urge to run and embrace Simeon, to hold him close and press her ear against his cheek, so she can hear the whispers contained in his head. She wonders if he is dreaming. What would he dream? She wants to reach out and touch him, draw the flick of hair away from his forehead. But she doesn't dare disturb him, if he wakes he will be difficult to calm. Sometimes, if she can't sleep, she sits in the armchair watching Simeon sleeping, smelling the warm fragrance of child, letting it drift over her as if she was a cat guarding her kitten.

But tonight she feels thirsty. Returning to the corridor she makes her way to the kitchen. She draws her dressing gown more tightly around her. The house feels strange tonight, the air charged and she is aware of the storm building outside. The day has been sultry pressing in on her giving her a headache. She knows animals portend storms and scurry to their burrows and dens. This is what she wants to do. Find somewhere safe. But everywhere appears to have the possibility of movement, as if she is living aboard a ship. As she pads into the kitchen, the rain clatters against the windows and the old frames rattle, so she can feel little draughts of air brushing against her. The wind rises and falls like the press of bellows and the strike and smatter of the rain make her think of sparks of fire. It is very dark and beneath the noise of the storm the house shivers and echoes. She can hear whispering as if the Isherwood ancestors have met to discuss the implication of their decision.

A crack of lightening forks the sky; outside she sees silhouettes. The interlude is brief, all returns to darkness and she cannot remember whether the shadows she saw were images of real things or alien visitors. She is not wearing her glasses and squints, unable to focus. Thunder rolls.

There is a movement behind her and she jumps, fear making her cold.

'What are you doing?' asks Ambrose, 'Couldn't you sleep?'

Kate's hand is at her throat trying to contain the fear. 'You scared me, creeping up like that.'

Another flash of lightening illuminates the kitchen, edging everything with a line of light. Again Kate is aware of the looming grotesques in the garden.

The kitchen is cold. Ambrose has never liked the house at night. It has too many dark nooks and crannies, where who knows what could hide. Momentarily, he thinks he has been transposed to his boyhood body. He realises he is being ridiculous. He is a scientist and should not give in to flights of fancy. But into his brain seeps the thought of dark matter. A mist of particles present and passing through him all the time. Matter able to travel deep within the valleys and dark places of the brain; a series of continuous and incomprehensible interactions. What if it can generate ghosts or is the essence of telepathy or prophecy. What if it is the creator of a soul? Would that make it God? He shakes his head against the unseen dark matter floating around him and tries to clear his head. He is obviously still half asleep, his mind is wandering. Looking at Kate in her long satin dressing gown, with her pale skin and wide eyes, he has the sudden notion she is a spectre and not real at all. She seems to float closer to the window as another crack of lightning strikes. She looks ephemeral in the illumination as if she could simply disappear. He moves beside her and puts his hand on her arm, confirming she is a living breathing mortal. Kate hears him sigh and wonders if he is cross with her for getting him out of bed. They watch the dark night, hearing thunder growl and the rain thrashing against the glass.

'Another storm. There have been so many recently.'

'Global warming.' Ambrose makes the statement, sure of the causative factor.

The seconds between thunder and lightning become shorter.

'It's getting closer,' Ambrose says, putting his arm around Kate's shoulders. She leans into him, feeling secure with him beside her.

Suddenly, there is a light like a helicopter spot light hanging above them, making the whole garden bright. The accompanying noise is so loud it sounds like rotors thrumming towards them. Then there is a scream, as if metal is cutting through metal. Flame is being drawn down the trunk of the copper beech, a laser line trailing flame and wrenching it in two. Then the darkness closes in leaving only a smouldering flicker in the night.

'My God. The beech!' Ambrose shouts.

There is a thud from the front of the house. Ambrose does not move. Kate screams, 'Simeon!' She turns and runs along the corridor, dreading what she might find, having just witnessed the destruction of the beech.

Simeon had been dreaming. His head full of vivid colours so intense his mind did not seem to have the space to contain them. He imagined the hues spreading out in bands across the dark room. A rattle accompanied the picture and he became a kaleidoscope rotating through geometry he has no concept of. Then there is a crash. He is awake. He has been torn apart, hurled from his bed. He feels as if he is in two segments, one lying in the bed and one on the floor, sensing the cold board pressing under his cheekbone.

Kate cannot move at the door of Simeon's room. She can't conceive what has happened. She is so frightened she is unable to transfer weight from one leg to the other. She has lifted a foot ready to be placed but has stopped as if there is a barrier to negotiate. She takes in the ragged shape of Simeon's body prone on the floor and the bed guard rails still in place. How can he have fallen?

'Simeon?' she whispers.

It starts quietly, the penetrative sound of an alarm at a distance, but then the scream sounds fully. Kate does not think she has ever heard Simeon screaming at such volume. Now she rushes to him and cradles him in her arms. 'Simeon, are you hurt?' she asks, stroking his hair, noticing its clammy texture.

Gradually Simeon senses the support of his mother and starts to calm.

A shadow hovers at the door, blocking the light falling over Kate and Simeon.

'Is he alright?' Ambrose asks.

'I think so.'

'Here, let me put him back to bed.'

Ambrose lifts Simeon as if he weighs nothing. He checks the bed rails. They stay for several minutes, watching Simeon fall back to sleep with little grunts and snuffles. Then they return to their own bed.

'What do you think can have happened?' Kate asks Ambrose, 'I found him on the floor. How can he have got there?'

Ambrose cannot answer. He does not have an answer. His thoughts are jumbled, his eyes still spotted with dark rimmed stars from the intensity of lightening striking the beech. Instead of certainty, he suddenly feels vulnerable. There are things he cannot fathom, forces beyond him that he cannot grasp.

'Ambrose?' questions Kate again, usually certain of a response.

'I don't know,' Ambrose says finally, finding the unfamiliar phrase uncomfortable on his lips, like coarse sand.

# X

Quarks, Leptons, Gluons, Higgs-Boson; man applies names to things. There is not yet a word that would encompass the entity or the effect it has. It existed before words. Nor does it have a name for its offspring. It is beyond words.

Ambrose is driving to work. For once he and Kate left at similar times. Driving into the Yorkshire countryside he feels released. The wind is blowing, grey clouds scudding and he remembers days like this when he would take a kite out to the pasture. Sometimes, his father or uncle would accompany him. He imagines Simeon holding the end of the string, listening to the music of the kite dancing into the distance and the thrum of its vibration. Ambrose senses the car moving along the twists in the road and smiles as he looks at the panorama before him. The green patchwork of the flood plain stretches upward toward the purple of hills. The tone changes depending on the hue of the sky. Today it is greys on greys but with sunlight fanning through in bands, cutting up the view into a cubist panorama of shadow and light and startling dimensions. The hills below are dusky and shadowed. When he turns the next bend, Ambrose will see the outline of the building. On grey rainy days the buildings are hardly visible. Those times are his favourite, when only as he gets closer does the outline become stronger, losing the mirage quality and becoming real. Today, where the sunlight touches them, they will be silvery, shimmering structures bounded by the amethyst of the moorland. Geometric shapes of steel; oblongs and cubes, like a baby's building blocks. As a child he'd had a box of bricks. Simple wooden geometric shapes, stained in different shades. He has the notion that he once constructed the vision of a building like this with his rectangles, arches and columns. The box is in the attic now; palaces, cities, research facilities, patiently awaiting construction. The set had been kept for his children to play with. But Simeon never will. 'Unless...' optimism sparks like that beam of sunlight and gives him hope that after the operation everything might be different.

Ambrose realises his hands are moist. The twists and turns of the road are familiar to him. He is used to the sense of excitement he always feels as he takes the corner of the next bend but he has an added thrill today.

His heart has an unfamiliar beat. He cannot remember the last time he was this nervous. He is even chewing some gum to make sure his breath does not smell. Acting like a schoolboy on his first date. And this is not a date. This is a proper scientific endeavour. Yet, you can't invite Mallory to the Research Facility without it turning into a media frenzy. Already, the usually sparse parking area is crawling with cars and fans, barriers and security guards.

As the lift descends Ambrose is aware for the first time of the drop in his stomach but realises it is simply the excitement of being confined in this space with Mallory by his side. Even though there are three other researchers, a reporter and cameraman in the lift, he feels cocooned with her. There is also a politician, whom he has almost forgotten. The man hunkers in the umbra of the cage, eclipsed totally by Mallory. Yet Ambrose knows it is this man he must impress. This man must understand the importance of the research project. The future of the Dark Matter programme rests with him. The man's hands are too large, protruding like shovels from his borrowed boiler suit. He imagines the hand fisting around a pot of money, crushing it to dust. Ambrose shivers, looks at Mallory again and smiles.

She looks wonderful, even the orange coveralls, which on most people look like sacking, enhance her figure. The hard hat does nothing to detract from her beauty. Also her perfume invades the space. His colleague Dougie actually has his eyes closed and is swaying with a smile of bliss on his face, as if he has been transported to paradise. Ambrose suspects they are all similarly affected, even Claire, the local reporter, appears starstruck. Mallory just has a mesmeric effect on people.

At a basic scientific level, Ambrose reasons that it is simply chemical reactions which achieve the charismatic effect. Glands, triggering responses of cells, sending impulses to other cells, ultimately creating the aura surrounding her. But scientists are yet to discover those precise reactions. He wonders if the prophets of old; Jesus, Muhammad, Buddha and Mahavira, were endowed with a similar magnetism. Was that why they were considered to be the offspring of gods?

The lift jolts to a halt and Mallory gives a giggle of surprise at the sudden bump. The sound flits and reverberates off the criss-cross struts of metal enclosing them. Dougie opens his eyes with a look of disbelief that he is not in Nirvana but at the bottom of a mineshaft. The doors slither open with a groan and more reluctance than usual. Immediately, the wall of damp soil invades his nostrils, so Ambrose feels suddenly bereft at the absence of Mallory's perfume.

Every movement down here echoes, so breathing and footsteps make them sound like the relentless marching of an army. The initial tunnel is dark and dusty, with the light from the helmet torches flickering off silver pipes above them, which seem to writhe like roots of alien trees.

Ambrose loves this bit of the journey underground, thinking about all the men who have travelled here before him, cutting out the coal. He can feel the mass of rock balanced above him, the press of it akin to an embrace. He knows he is safe here.

Mallory asks, 'What are you actually trying to find?' Ambrose is aware of the politician's feet pattering beside him, struggling to keep up with the longer strides of him and Mallory.

'WIMPs,' Ambrose replies, and he can't help but give a sidelong look at the politician beside him. In the subdued lighting he senses a complicit smile on Mallory's lips and returns the gesture, enjoying a sense of a joke shared.

'What does that stand for then?' she continues.

'Weakly Interacting Massive Particles. They're particles we can't see but expect must be in the atmosphere because of the way planets act.'

'Why down here though? It's really deep down, innit?'

'It's quiet. Not from noise, but from all the other particles that would be present if we were at ground level.'

They progress towards a well-lit space where they put on white clean-room suits and make their way into the main laboratory, with its gleaming copper and stainless steel apparatus, computer stations and wires of different dimensions. Ambrose takes pleasure in seeing Mallory reflected from every surface as though the instruments were conspiring to multiply her.

Ambrose talks them through the lines on computer screens; the idea of trying to capture the enigmatic particles, which he knows must exist.

'What we're looking for is the reaction of the WIMPs with an atom of Xenon. When that happens there is a flash, which leaves a trail. That's what we measure.'

Ambrose thinks about the reactions as glow worms lighting up a dark vista. He recalls forays on the edge of the forest with his uncle. He still senses a shudder of excitement at the recollection of the adventure into the pitch night. They would switch their torches off when they reached the edge of the trees. As there was no light pollution, the air was a magical cloak of ink covering them. He can't remember any noise; the sky turned above them in silence and the trees were still. Even his breathing was shallow as if walking through a dreamscape. Stars shone so brightly they appeared almost touchable, and his uncle had explained they were so far away that the light was only just reaching them, years and years later, so long ago that the star might have died.

Gradually, the darkness would be embellished by dew drops of light as glow worms danced. Ambrose smiles at the warmth of the memory. Uncle Rex had explained the chemical reaction of luciferin, oxidised into oxyluciferin, a bioluminescence so sophisticated and efficient it eclipses humanity's feeble struggle at instant light. How could you fail to be amazed at the evolution of such a brilliant device? And for what? For the chance to reproduce. The female would only live for twelve days, but those days were vital in maintaining the glowworm lineage. Although elusive, the glowworm could still be found in England. Ambrose makes a vow that he will search for them again. With Simeon.

It takes time for him to return to the present. The politician's voice is pricking the air.

'Have you actually found any of these things though? This 'dark matter'?'

The politician's voice is so quiet he has to repeat the question twice. In fact Ambrose hears him the first time but doesn't want to answer because, in over a decade, they have yet to find anything significant. He ignores the actual question and replies, 'Here we have been instrumental in developing the most sensitive apparatus. We are world leaders in this area.'

'But have you found 'the matter'?' the politician persists.

'Well,' Ambrose pauses, 'we're nearly there. We could make a break through any day.' But he can see from the man's expression that he has just put a mental bold red line through 'the matter' experiment.

The rest of the session moves sluggishly, as if he is wading through deep water. Ambrose knows he can do nothing to impress this man, who is likely to remove government funding, meaning the research project will have to close. When bending to remove the clean-room suit before returning to the surface he becomes dizzy and leans on the wall for a moment. It is draining to watch all his work seep away because of a man in a poorly fitted suit.

Mallory puts a hand on his shoulder, 'What's up, Rambo? Are you alright?'

If they were alone, he might have turned and embraced her, crying that it wasn't fair. Not after all the time and effort that had been put into the research. It would be soothing to be embraced in her warm arms and smell her perfume. He could ask her out, discuss when he could see her again. But they weren't alone. Nor was this a celebrity jungle where Mallory could address him in that stupid way.

'I'm fine thank you, Mallory,' he says, standing up to his full height, 'just stumbled over my suit.' And taking a deep breath so that any hint of tears is vacuumed away he says, 'Now let's get out of here.'

# XI

The beginning of any experiment is very simple. A basic equation. There is a starting point, then a reaction, which leads to an outcome. But depending on your knowledge, it might be impossible to believe the starting point and outcome are connected. And equations are man-made. They are how we try to interpret the unknown. How the entity starts its experiment will never be understood by the human race, unless their brain capacity increases, something which has not changed in nearly two hundred thousand years. Let's just accept it will never be known.

Following their discussion with the surgeon about the operation, Kate's dreams have disturbed her. She wanders strange mansions and finds sewing boxes stuffed with thread she cannot untangle. Clumps of vivid cottons unwind in red and violet, captured within broken zips with jagged teeth. Pincushions lurk in dark corners with their hypodermic spikes.

Since Monday, the dreams have an added edge, played against a backdrop of newspaper print and beautiful creatures dressed in orange.

She is surprised that it has taken so long for her to find out. It is the sort of revelation she would expect her mother to deliver, arriving flourishing the newspaper and slapping it down onto the kitchen table with a 'What did I tell you,' or simply a look that meant 'I told you so,' without the necessity of speech. But perhaps Norma didn't read the type of paper where this kind of celebrity story lurked.

No, it had been at work. Kate had taken a moment with a cup of coffee and flicked through a colleague's newspaper. In a column called 'People News!' there was the photograph. Her first thought was how beautiful Mallory managed to look in orange coveralls. It was seconds later she realised the 'Prof' referred to in the headline was Ambrose, and it took a further moment for the realisation that he had invited Mallory to the research project to sink in. They smiled at her from the photograph, looking contented and comfortable together. The information took a long time to digest. By the time it had filtered through that Ambrose had invited Mallory to the mine, without saying a word to her, Kate's coffee had gone cold.

Her colleague returned and looked over Kate's shoulder. 'She's lovely, isn't she? Not got two brain cells to rub together, but still gorgeous. She and Ambrose look very cosy.'

By the time she returned to the lab she was still no clearer on what to do. Instruments jangled against each other. The contents of vials and test tubes looked garish and the winking of lights on the computers made her eyes ache. Perhaps that was why there was a film of tears preparing to spill from her. All afternoon, through the clatter and hum of the lab, a thought had buzzed in her brain, not exactly a thought but a question. The question: 'Should she say anything to Ambrose?'

There has been an accident on the by-pass as Kate makes her way home. The usual rush-hour traffic is bumper-to-bumper. As she inches forward, shoe to brake, shoe to clutch robotically, she comes to a decision. She will say nothing.

Kate is sitting on the stool in front of her dressing table. She is almost ready for bed, just finishing brushing her hair. It lifts with static as she runs the bristles through it.

Ambrose is still in his study; she can't hear him but knows he is there. She won't say anything to him about Mallory but she feels different around him and wonders whether he noticed over supper. She hardly dares say anything in case the name, 'Mallory', falls out of her mouth, followed by spittle and accusation and tears. Ambrose has never been comfortable with what he calls 'histrionics'.

They've discussed before the root of the word 'hysterical', from the Greek word for uterus. She puts her palms flat against her belly and imagines her own womb atrophying now she is approaching the menopause. At the thought, she feels a flush spreading from beneath her fingers and rising upwards, making her skin tingle. She looks at her face in the mirror; it has taken on a red tinge. This is a symptom she has noticed increasingly often.

Looking at her three blushing reflections she annunciates the name. '*Mallory. Mallory. Mallory.*' She turns her head to address each image individually.

The triplets respond with moving mouths that don't make a sound. Kate knows the images are not real. In fact, they are less than real; they have no depth or dimension. They are created because of light falling on a surface capable of reflection... That reflected light causes a series of reactions on cells at the back of her eyes and then along nerve pathways into her brain, which informs her of what she sees. The image has even been inverted through one hundred and eighty degrees. Does this suggest she exists in a world that is really upside down? Kate has difficulty solving her own conundrum and also accepting the flatness of the reflections, because they appear to be feeling what she is, she can see the lines of worry on their faces.

Ambrose is pacing in his study, looking at a letter in his hand. It is from the funding body that has been supporting his research. It will not be doing so for much longer. The signature on the bottom of the letter is a mess of lines, like a child's scribble. He is barely able to make out the letters of the name. It is the impotence that makes him most angry, that he can do nothing about this unfair decision. 'Just a bit more time', he wants to shout. But there is nobody to plead with. He thumps his fist on the desk top, appreciating the vibration that thrums through his flesh, making the contours of wood appear to ripple. Looking out at his stricken beech tree, Ambrose thinks the leaves tremble and senses that it perceives his mood, as if there is an empathetic droop to its branches. The tint of the hills deepens to purple fists behind it. The sky above is clear for once, and Ambrose is soothed by the expanse of the darkening sky, where the first stars are visible. The lines from a song drift into his head, 'We are stardust, billion year old carbon.' The thought settles him. Ancient stars, which may no longer exist by the time the light reaches earth, helium bonding as the stars die, making carbon that has formed the earth, formed the people on it. The thought is so vast is takes over every other sensation he feels, his frustration and anger dwindle in the knowledge of such power.

Kate can hear a strange sound, like the movement of a fan. Behind the mirror she finds a butterfly, its wings ragged as though it has been trapped in a dusty corner. It unsettles her. A butterfly should not be indoors. She looks at it more closely, as it drags itself across the dressing table. It is definitely a butterfly, its colour and wing shape unmistakable. It should not be here. She wonders if it will survive if she releases it outside. She puts out her hand for it to crawl upon. But it finds energy and flaps away towards the light bulb. A voice in her head murmurs about the butterfly effect, and she knows she must treat the creature with care. A wrong move could cause a catastrophe. She shudders as the butterfly falls and drops in front of her. A pile of dust.

In his bed, Simeon briefly opens his eyes and whimpers. In his dream he had been floating, his body had felt comfortable and warm as if he were supported by a huge hand lifting him gently. Then thump. He had been dropped back into his bed so his body again was awkward. But now everything is quiet and calm again. He shuts his eyes and goes back to sleep.

# XII

And so the Earth turns. Our position rotating in and out of the light of the Sun—day following night. Humanity tries to constrain time by inventing dials, and cogs and clocks. We mark the years and months; weeks, hours and days. Fill the minutes with matters we believe important. Trying to make sense of this short life on Earth. But the entity is outside the constraints of time or space.

They have been sitting in the garden with Norma. It's a late September afternoon with the sun now low in the sky. Kate knows she should move before Simeon gets cold. As a concession, she reaches out and straightens the rug over his knees.

Simeon senses the fabric move across his limbs, and smiles. The touch of the blanket is warm whereas a breeze has made his cheeks cool. He is smiling as the air moves around him, stroking his face, lifting his hair, making tickles and trembles through his whole body, as if he is central to its movement, fundamental to the rhythm of its dance. Today he is aware of a change to the air. The smell is different now, he can taste its ripeness on his lips and saliva dribbles onto his chin.

Ambrose watches the spider thread of spittle trailing from Simeon's mouth. He should wipe it away but he feels listless. He is tired. His thoughts flit from Mallory to Simeon and back again.

'Have another piece of cake,' Norma says.

He has already eaten two slices, the chocolate sticks in the corners of his mouth. His stomach feels bloated. All afternoon Norma's nagging has disrupted his train of thought repeatedly. He has to revisit each previous idea as if re-reading an interrupted paragraph. Simeon's operation looms towards him, Mallory, a mere shadow of desire in the background.

He wanders off down the garden before Norma insists Ambrose eats a third piece of cake. He sees the look of panic Kate throws at him as he departs, but ignores it.

The changing season soothes him. The trees are laced with bronze filigree edging the darker canopies. The September sunlight slants through the indigo striations of evening cloud. It melts over the hills turning them gold. This transformation reminds him of the ancient alchemists who tried to transmute base metals into gold. He knows that formation of heavier elements takes place in stars late in their cycle, in their often-violent deaths. Despite their long history, the alchemists became heretics in the eyes of the Church. It was Galileo who observed the heliocentric model of the solar system, suggesting that the Earth rotated round the Sun. The puppet not the master. Four hundred years ago, this theory was so shocking that Galileo ended up accused of heresy. Ambrose wonders whether, if he discovered a concept that revolutionary about dark matter, would he be equally persecuted. The idea releases a faint thrill down his spine.

And was it Galileo who commented that the Sun ripened grapes, as if it had nothing else in the universe to do? Ambrose is aware of the silent cycle of the seasons, the natural world, the Universe doing what it does, whatever the troubles of the people fretting on planet earth. Even the beech tree is starting to recover. The scar is black, the edges peeled back, revealing the tree's softer flesh. But it will mend. He looks towards the house and the dimming sun haloing Simeon's small figure. Perhaps he can be mended as well. It is not impossible.

He breathes the odour of change, the warmth of late summer mellowing into the ripeness of autumn. Gradually his shoulders relax as if he was a tree, the weight of leaves falling from him. Now he has the potential for renewal. With his equilibrium recovered he turns to walk back up the garden. A conker lies on the ground; green and spiked. He bends and picks it up.

Above him, on the terrace, Norma and Kate appear not to have moved. Simeon is tilting his head in sharp little movements, cocking it one way and then the other as if watching a tennis match. Perhaps Kate has told Norma about Simeon's operation. The tension returns to his shoulders and he begins to toss the chestnut from palm to palm. The prickles of its casing jab his skin.

Kate's saliva tastes sour, a bitter aftertaste in her mouth, which the chocolate cake does nothing to relieve. Kate's birthday has been and gone. It would have passed like a bump in the road; something to be negotiated and forgotten if it hadn't been for Norma's continued insistence that it must be celebrated. The cake is not a belated birthday cake made with affection, more like a rebuttal. When Norma arrived she thumped the cake down on the table so that the sharp knife beside it trembled and glinted in the afternoon sunshine. Her words accompanying the action were similarly edged, 'Don't you be having any cake, Katherine. I really made it for Ambrose, he looks so drawn lately.'

If there is such a thing as an unbirthday cake, Kate supposes that this is it.

The cake is Kate's favourite. Iced with butter cream, thick and delectable, scattered flakes of chocolate snuggle into its surface. A comforting aroma emanates from it, reminding her of days at home when she would make cakes with her mother and lick the bowl clean, before the fear of salmonella in raw egg, before she watched her waistline, before she didn't celebrate her birthday.

Perhaps the cake is why she hasn't told Norma about Simeon's operation. She meant to, but with the sweetness of butter icing, creamy in her mouth, she feels angry with Norma. Why would she bring a cake and then suggest Kate doesn't eat it? She knows Kate will be unable to resist, so instead of the cake sliding down with pleasure, it is accompanied by the bitter spittle of failure which catches in her throat.

As Ambrose joins them, it is obvious nothing has been said. Kate avoids his gaze, Norma smiles at him and says she must leave. As she stands, the low sunlight lengthens her shadow, and Kate thinks that's how tall Norma should be. Not a petite five feet four, but an imposing height to match her character. She watches as Norma reaches up to embrace Ambrose, leaning into him and kissing him on both cheeks. Not air kisses, but pecks that leave a moist imprint of her mouth on his flesh. Ambrose recoils slightly at the sticky sensation and Norma's sharp perfume, which fills his nostrils and obscures the garden aromas.

As Norma leaves, he presses his thumb into the flesh of the fruit. He knows it will not be ripe but feels the skin tear in his hand, bleeding acrid juice. The nut inside is ivory and seems to regard him not as something newborn, but blind, like a rheumy eye.

He drops it and slumps into his chair. Looking across at Kate he wants to ask what she has said to Norma. But she has closed her eyes and her posture is hunched, her arms crossed tightly, as if she is trying to mimic a tortoise retreating into its shell. She has shut him and everything out. If he speaks, he doesn't think she will answer.

Kate had thought Ambrose would say something. They had discussed it beforehand, saying it would be a good opportunity to fill Norma in about their plans for Simeon. But Ambrose has remained silent on the subject. When there had been a lull in the conversation and she thought he might broach it, he had made an excuse and gone to look at the garden. Then, instead of saying anything, he allowed Norma to get up and leave.

He'd pretended to be interested in a horse chestnut fruit that he stabbed viciously with his thumb. The undeveloped conker was a glossy albino mutant. It reminded Kate of the jars of pickled embryos and body parts which lurked in the shadowy laboratory shelves where she had done her degree. There were strange teratomas embalmed in amber fluid, the thick glass exaggerating their disfigured limbs. On the breeze, the scent of the maturing garden resembles the tang of formaldehyde, and she'd shuddered as Ambrose threw the conker on the ground. It rolled under Simeon's chair, resembling a miniature skull, regarding her with hollowed orbits. She closed her eyes, trying to shut the image out.

Ambrose bends from his chair and plucks a dandelion clock growing in the cracks of the paving. Absently he puts it to his mouth and blows just as he has done from childhood. 'One.' A few seeds spill from the globe and scatter. 'Two, three...' At each puff of breath more fall away until it is denuded. 'It's four o'clock. Time for tea.'

'I think your clock's wrong,' replies Kate, stirring in her chair and squinting across at him. She reaches down to grasp a seed head. She blows gently against the lace of its surface and watches as the seeds disperse like tiny parasols twirling across the garden.

Ambrose blows another clock towards Simeon. 'What do you think Simeon? Can you see the dandelion seeds?' The down brushes against Simeon's cheek like gentle raindrops. It tickles and he laughs.

'Each of those can grow into another dandelion plant if they land in the right place. That's why they're built to float on the breeze, so they can find a good place to grow... We could have a garden full of dandelions. How would you like that?'

Kate has closed her eyes again. She responds with a drowsy, 'I don't think Fran would be very pleased. He's struggling to keep the weeds under control with this warm and wet weather. They love it.'

Behind her lids is a warm orange glow; shaded shapes flicker, moving like silhouetted characters on a screen. She wonders if they are random or whether they are playing out an alternate reality. She would like to remain here, watching these players, knowing Ambrose and Simeon are close by. While she sits here she feels safe from the changes looming, as if being still confers protection. As in a game of grandmother's footsteps, she is immune.

Kate knows that when she opens her eyes she will see the crockery piled up on the tray and it will remind her that she should clear the things away. She keeps her eyes closed, squeezing them more tightly so the shadows darken and dance. She thinks about the dandelion seeds floating away, finding a good place to grow and wishes she could somehow be removed, cocooned, and float into the future. Towards a good place.

Suddenly, her thoughts are jarred. Knock, knock, knock. Simeon's foot against his chair. It sounds impatient. She worries he is getting cold.

This time next month everything will be different. However hard Kate concentrates she knows she is counting the days, minutes and seconds to that point. Simeon's knocking seems to accentuate the inevitability of this.

Simeon's foot strikes the metal of the chair. He is not impatient. He does not have a destination to look forward to; he does not look back at the past. He lives without time. *Bang, bang, bang...* His foot kicks, generating a slight tremble upwards through his bones; he is aware of having limbs.

Kate cannot bear the metronomic beat of Simeon's kicking. She opens her eyes. The white crockery gleams at her. She capitulates and takes the tray inside.

Looking down, Ambrose sees the torn shell of the conker. His fingers still retain the acrid slime from the skin. When he had walked to the bottom of the garden he had thought it would give Kate the opportunity to tell Norma, but watching her turn away and take the tray inside, he knows that she has not. He looks at the shell, ghost-like under the shadows of Simeon's chair and sighs.

# XIII

The entity is moving like a far-flung pebble. Plunging into deep space causing ripples of energy. Not in the concentric circular motion we would see if a stone fell in a pond but in a distorted way as if pitched into the sea, a disruption in the water but not interrupting the build-up of waves.

'Marietta, we need to talk to you.' Marietta continues to put cups in the cupboard, using the open door to shield her face from them. Even Simeon appears to be in on the conspiracy because he is quiet, thoughtful. All three of them are watching her.

'Marietta. Please come and sit down.'

There is a note of impatience in the voice. Marietta wonders how long she can resist the words that she knows are coming. She can hear the next 'M' of Marietta humming towards her like a threat and reluctantly shuts the cupboard door. Its soft-close suction colludes with them, instead of slamming with indignation.

Kate is at her side. 'Come on Marietta, it's really important.'

Ambrose has pulled a chair out for Marietta. She sits down hard and is satisfied it gives a little squeal of resistance as she pulls it towards the table. Ambrose and Kate have taken two seats opposite her, as if they are going to interrogate her.

'Marietta, we'd like you to take some time off.'

So, this is how they want to play it, Marietta thinks. As if nothing is going on, as if this plan has nothing to do with me.

'I don't need any time off, Mr Isherwood, I enjoy coming to work, being with Simeon.'

Kate has been sitting on her hands, she is convinced that if she manages to keep them under control, she will be able to keep quiet while Ambrose talks. But she is still waiting for Ambrose to explain the situation. He is hedging round the subject. 'Get to the point,' she wants to shout. They continue to watch Marietta, Marietta continues to stare back at them. Stand off. Finally, Kate can't keep her hands steady any more. She slaps them palm down on the table so they all jump. Words spill out of her mouth.

'Well, Simeon isn't going to be needing you for a while. He's going to have an operation, an operation to make him better, so you don't need to come in and look after him for the present, not while he's in hospital, which might be for a few weeks, we don't really know at the moment, no, we don't really know.' Kate finds it hard to stop but can't think of what else needs to be said. Then she takes a deep breath. She remembers. 'Oh, just some light cleaning maybe.'

Marietta's gaze has turned to look directly at Kate, as if she is mad.

'You want Simeon to have an operation?'

'Yes, yes, that's right.' Kate replies. Her thoughts feel swimmy, as if she is fixed and the room is spinning round them.

Finally Ambrose speaks, and the revolving walls slow.

'It has been a very difficult decision, Marietta, but an opportunity we've decided we must take, for Simeon's sake. I hope you'll support us in this. Would you like me to explain what is going to happen?'

Marietta shakes her head, a slow swing from side to side as if her head really isn't sure what to do. Her mind is full of questions and arguments, all of which she knows will be useless against Mr Isherwood. If it had just been Mrs Isherwood then she might have had a chance.

She realises there are tears in her eyes, ready to spill out. She sniffs.

'Marietta, I know this must be difficult for you, but as I say, this is in the best interests of Simeon. You know we appreciate the work you do here. So think of it as a little holiday. A paid holiday.'

Kate can't watch Marietta's face folding in on itself. A tear has run down her cheeks like a marble bouncing down a bagatelle board, unsure of where it will stop. She thinks if she watches any longer she will start to cry too. She gets up to put the kettle on.

With her back to Marietta and Ambrose, looking at the green of the garden soothes her. Simeon's reflection in the glass appears as a mirage in the garden. He remains silent.

'Let me do that, Mrs Isherwood,' Marietta pushes by her to get cups out. 'You go and sit back down.' But Kate doesn't think she wants to sit; only movement will curb the agitation she feels inside. She glances out of the window; a magpie flies in, its black and white wings striking through the air like knives. It lands by the feet of the reflected Simeon. 'One for sorrow,' Kate says, more loudly than she usually does, and touches her collar. She would feel much happier if there had been two birds. 'Good morning, Mr Magpie,' she voices, unable to stop herself repeating the phrase which will offer her protection against any malign influences the bird brings. She knows it is irrational to believe in such superstitions but she can't help her reaction. She thinks she hears Marietta tutting at her side, getting cups out.

'It's just a bird, Mrs Isherwood,' Marietta says fiercely, 'Just a bird.'

Kate can sense the scorn in Marietta's comment. She imagines Marietta's head full of unspoken words of mockery, tumbling against each other with derision, like bullies in a playground. The sensation is so intense that Kate lifts her hands to her head to stop her own thoughts from lurching about.

'Are you alright, Mrs Isherwood?' Marietta asks her, but Kate believes even this is spoken with contempt.

'Yes, yes, I'm fine,' Kate replies, 'Just a bit of a headache coming on.'

The magpie appears to watch her. It hops across the grass, trampling on Simeon's reflection with its clawed feet. The bird's beady eyes seem to fix on her as if it is deliberately intending to agitate her. As the kettle boils, steam rises and objects on the shelf vibrate, producing the sensation of a miniature earthquake. Steam condenses the windowpane cloudy, obscuring the image of Simeon. But the magpie is still visible, seeping into the film of moisture like ink on blotting paper. Perhaps Marietta is right to be cautious; perhaps they are about to make a terrible mistake.

# XIV

Time is humanity's creation, not the entity's. The entity moves as it pleases, twisting through different dimensions without constraint or concern. Man sees the sunrise and the sunset and imagines a pattern of days and seasons and years. But the entity is timeless. If man imagines that time is like a string then it is the entity, which tugs and tangles it, playing with the planets like a puppeteer.

It is only two weeks until the operation. Why Ambrose has chosen to stay away from home at this point Kate does not know. He is on a lecture tour of universities, which was booked months ago. But he could have postponed it. The idea makes her swallow; she can taste the bitterness of her thoughts in her gullet, as she suspects he might be staying away because of Mallory.

'You could have said that you couldn't attend for family reasons,' she had suggested. Ambrose simply replied that he could not let them down.

She has looked up the lecture schedule on the university website and, if it were not for Simeon, she might have followed Ambrose secretly. She visualises herself in mac and fedora crouching in shadows beneath gothic arches, like a gumshoe. Never before has this impulse filled her head, the desire to spy on Ambrose. But the force is so strong that she gets a holdall out of the wardrobe and considers what she should take, before she realises what she's doing and stops.

In the early hours of the morning the bed is like a shipwreck, as if it is unbalanced by the absence of Ambrose's ballast and has been tossed and twisted in a storm.

Kate hardly sleeps, briefly slips into unconsciousness where she is immersed in dreams of strange sea creatures and mermaids who look like Mallory.

As the dawn lifts she lies and watches light creep through the gaps of the curtains and create a geometry of shapes across the ceiling. She feels hot and the bedding is damp. The sweat on her face tastes salty.

The patterns above her change as the dawn develops into day. She senses her own metamorphosis but hers is less geometrical, more organic. Her body is tired, her skin sagging and drying and, inside, her organs shrivelling. It is the opposite of adolescent blooming and equally disturbing. Yet she knows she must change. A world without change is one of stagnation. And maybe Simeon must change too.

Simeon, lying in his bed, has no concept of change. Cells within his subconscious brain, which constitute a biological clock, simply rouse him at six a.m. He will expect movement because that is what always occurs. A wet cloth will be wiped across his face, so he will blink and shake his head. Granules of sleep dust will be swept from the corners of his eyes, so he will press them tightly shut. A comb will drag over his head, lifting his fine hair, and he will sense the crackle of static electricity in a halo above him. Sometimes it tickles and makes him giggle. Then his limbs will be lifted and massaged before cool, fresh clothing covers his body. But today his body senses delay. Things have happened, but nothing has begun. One of his legs kicks out striking the metal of the bed guard, sounding a chord. Simeon likes the noise. He does not know how to generate it again.

Kate listens to the alarm buzz for the fifth time and knows she must get up. She feels tired and lethargic, her heavy limbs reluctant to stir. Two weeks is all they have.

They have been waiting so long. All of Simeon's life, certainly. Perhaps all her own life, which stretches behind her like a counting string with its knots marking significant events. The thought of it makes her sense she is pulling and twisting that cord between her fingers, making them raw.

Looking down she sees her hands are twisted together. Over the last few months the passage of time has been unpredictable; sometimes the days seem endless and at others slip by rapidly. Kate realises they are approaching the brink. But it is as if she can't grab hold of a point in time, that next important knot in the cord. Forever, everything else in their lives will be measured before or after that event.

# XV

Some people would say that being a parent is the most important job in the world. For humans, it is closer to being a creator than anything else. But the power that accompanies it comes with anxiety. And, as with mortal parents, the entity hopes for its child to be more than the sum of its forebears.

Ambrose is listening to the sound of the train wheels below him. He is comfortable in his first class seat, his eyes partly drawn to the cryptic crossword and partly to the countryside rushing past. The momentum and rumble of the train around him is making him sleepy. He remembers the original pulsing of the steam trains he used to love. He can recall the powerful pistons dancing with a precision which fascinated him. It was akin to the sound of his mother's heart beating when she embraced him. He was very small when steam drifted away to be replaced by diesel trains but it is those days that are among his earliest memories. An image of himself standing on a platform with Uncle Rex hovers in his head. A sudden rush and clattering sound and he is engulfed in smoky steam. It is dense with soot. He cannot see; the cloud blinds him. For a moment he is terrified, the world has disappeared. Uncle Rex has been swallowed by the smog monster. Never before has he felt so alone. Then gradually Uncle Rex and the world are released, they emerge piecemeal from the cloud and Ambrose just feels changed, as if the steam has embedded within his body, choosing him. After that, he demands Uncle Rex takes him to the station every week so he can watch the trains close up. He has a pocket book somewhere with all the numbers written down. In 1975, having recently graduated from Cambridge, he actually attended the opening of the Railway Museum in York. Even then he'd had a yearning for taking a son around the displays, pointing out the wondrous engines, then explaining the concepts of the internal combustion engine.

The crossword solutions evade him, the black and white squares swim at him. He rubs his eyes, realising just how tiring the lectures were, particularly the polite chit-chat afterwards. Words that meant nothing.

The constant rhythm of the train makes him think about time. He remembers something somebody once said, 'We always live in the past.' The person was referring to delays while a sense organ converts stimuli into nerve impulses and while the brain receives; analyses and interprets the information. Only after that does one consciously see, hear or taste. But it's not the only reason he lives in the past; the future is making him anxious.

Kate has burnt the toast again and the smell suffuses the kitchen. She opens the back window and hurls the blackened slabs as far as she can. They splat onto the grass beyond the patio. Two pigeons, their grey chests puffed, investigate as if patrolling the area for suspect missiles.

Simeon can smell something alien. He can taste it as he breathes in. It is not a pleasant sensation and makes him choke.

Kate comes over to him, 'Sorry, Sweetheart.' She is distracted as she wipes his face, so the cloth covers his eyes and for a second he is blinded, locked within a cloud of singed air. He starts to cough and Kate apologises again.

Ambrose comes into the house, pauses in the gunroom, drops his bag, removes his coat and goes into the kitchen. Both Kate and Simeon appear to be staring into space. When he closes the door, Kate turns towards him, but she looks through him, rather than at him. For a second he wonders if he is still on the train and is merely imagining his homecoming. The odour of burnt toast makes him consider that he has been engulfed by his childhood memory of steam and, instead of being delivered on the platform with Uncle Rex, he has taken a step in a different direction and ended up in this kitchen, in an alternate dimension.

'Hi,' he says, pleased that the word sounds real, rebounding off the walls, ceiling and furniture. Kate has her back towards him, having turned to look out of the window again. Ambrose continues, adding a bright chivvying tone to his voice, 'How is everybody?' And then when there is no response he asks, 'Are you alright? Is Simeon alright?' He turns in Simeon's direction, in case it is Simeon who is unwell. But Simeon shows no sign of distress, in fact he is calm and still for once. There is no dribble on his face. Ambrose strides across the kitchen and embraces Kate, but she turns so that his lips brush her cheek, rather than her mouth. He feels accused of some misdemeanour but does not know what, or how to resolve it. On previous occasions Kate has shown understanding of his need to carry out public engagements, especially on the lecture circuit.

'Kate?' he questions again, hoping to get her attention, but she is still looking out of the window. Finally she says, 'The rooks seem agitated,' and Ambrose thinks she is announcing this to the room rather than him. He stands beside her and watches the birds circling the treetops. Indeed they do look restless. 'I think there're more storms coming.' Kate says, and does not appear to need a reply. Ambrose loosens his tie and makes his way out of the room and up to his study.

# XVI

The entity is searching. It glides across galaxies, slides into our solar system, drawn by a pinprick of light. There is a warp here, a bulge in the fabric of whichever dimension it seeks and it is curious. Here is something differentiated which distorts space. An enigma which may be the source of a cure.

Simeon recognises something is different this morning. He has been transported in a bus like the school bus, but has not arrived there. He is in a room with more people than usual, talking in hushed tones. The whispers float in his head, tickling his thoughts. He can hear rain in the background pattering against the windowpane. When he turns his head the raindrops refract the light, splitting it into spectrums of colour that shift in front of him. He allows his eyes to dance with the movement of miniature rainbows reflected on the walls. If he concentrates they imprint on his retinas and he feels his senses absorb the colours, making him tingle all over. It is such a peaceful sensation he does not want it to stop. 'Mmm,' he says.

Kate is trembling. she doesn't know if the tremor is visible to the others in the room. Her anxiety vibrates deep in her bones like the start of an earthquake. The epicentre is at her core, about to shatter her. The conversation revolves around her in waves. She cannot concentrate. At least Simeon looks calm. She looks at Ambrose for support but he is looking away, watching light scatter around the room. She thinks that he is probably working out the angles of refraction and wishes she had something definite to cling to.

Ambrose looks at the spectrum created by the raindrops and marvels at the light refracting through them. The sun, giving colour to the world. He considers the range of visible light, wavelengths from four hundred to seven hundred nanometres. Long waves of red, shorter of violet.

And then all the other wavelengths the human eye cannot see, X-rays, microwaves, gamma rays and maybe many more that are as yet undiscovered.

Kate wants to reach out and touch Ambrose but daren't when he seems so distant from her. She imagines his warm hand steadying her quaking. But he continues to stare at the splitting light.

Kate cannot breathe, her heart judders, her skin is clammy. She expects this is what it might feel if she were descending to her own execution. All morning rain has continued to pour down. It hammers in her head, a constant drumming that seems to repeat, 'What are you doing? What are you doing…?'

The lower floor of the research building has been remodelled from a surgical research unit for animals, to a hospital room for Simeon.

The clinic looks functional, polished steel with a hospital smell. But Kate knows this is a facade. Her son is to be experimented on like one of the lab animals. She thinks of Nazi experiments in dark cellars.

There are documents to sign, endless sheets of paper to read and then mark, stating she is prepared to throw Simeon's life away if that is what occurs. Her hand quakes as she signs.

Ambrose's signature is firmer. They have not spoken this morning. Ambrose senses the need to retain all their energy simply to get through the day. He is aware of Kate trembling beside him like a caged animal. He daren't touch her for fear she might collapse. And he feels if he speaks, his words might make him fragment like a tower with unstable foundations.

The sound of the pen scratches over the rough surface of the paper. All that needed to be said, has been said. They cannot go back. Before he was wheeled away, consumed by the dim corridor, Kate touched Simeon's hand and whispered, 'I love you'. She wishes he had responded, been able to acknowledge the remark.

Simeon appeared remarkably calm that morning, unaware of the experiment he is about to undergo. In fact, Simeon sensed the change in atmosphere. Instead of the rush around him on usual mornings, today has been silent and ordered. Everybody is touching him, but the touches are different. He sensed it was a day when nothing might happen, or something. But he is not at school today and that makes it good.

The noises around him are not those of home, or of school. The sound of his chair and voices ring and reverberate longer so he senses he is surrounded by waves. He sways his body in an arrhythmic dance. The voices and smells are no longer familiar. The odour, like the sound, is sharper and clearer. He does not worry. He is quite comfortable here. It is warm.

Marietta is cleaning. She has been given time off and doesn't know what to do. She has spent all day cleaning her house and now is standing by the sink again. There is nothing to wash up and the net curtains are clean so light filters through the embroidered pattern onto the soap in the basin. She watches the light flicker over the suds in the bowl, amazed at their iridescence. She is mesmerised by the ever-changing glisten of purple, green and blue smeared over the shiny surface. She must keep moving, if she does not she is sure she will explode. Every so often she takes a sniff and when she wipes her nose with her handkerchief, she is surprised there are tears running down her face. She has no mechanism with which to stop them, as if there is a leaking washer in the construction of her eyes. She even phoned her daughter but haltingly made up a stupid request, saying, 'When are you coming to visit?'

When she tried to speak, rather than pour out her feelings about Simeon's operation, she was dumb. She has been forbidden to talk about it. She sinks her hands into the water. Below the suds the water is scalding but she keeps her hands plunged in as if only the removal of her skin will cleanse them. Somehow she has the Isherwoods' sin on her hands.

'Have mercy on us...' she prays.

Simeon feels as if he is floating. A leaf on a breeze. But he is not the leaf; he is the breeze, moving without restraint. He has no body to bind him, no flailing limbs he cannot control. He is at one with the Universe; without beginning, without end.

The elements of his body have been teased apart to the tiniest of particles, the building blocks of life itself. And now  he moves like a breath. A whisper that can be heard by everything. He has no limits.

Suddenly the sensation stops. A barrier has fallen around him, caging him. He is not in a cage, but he is the constraint. Hard, heavy, bounded.

He is trapped.

# XVII

The entity does not appreciate the disturbance it makes investigating our solar system as it forays nearer to Earth. It flutters on the edge of human existence, creating a butterfly effect. Matter swells and diffuses, so sunspots and solar flares become more frequent. On Earth, the atmosphere responds with storms and tempests. If people were able to use their thoughts as the animal world does, they might perceive the magnetic alteration and take action. Hunkering down like beasts of the field.

It might have been raining forever; the sky is filled with it, the garden saturated in it. Kate sees only grey haze as she looks out of the kitchen window. It appears limitless. There is no change between sky and horizon, each blurs into the other like the smudging on a charcoal drawing. The hills are a distant cloudy blur of darkness set against louring cumulus; the copper beech is a black shroud.

The rain strikes unrelenting onto the garden, leaching colour from the once vibrant foliage. It should sound loudly but clings to the windowpane without noise. Kate's hands on the ceramic white of the kitchen sink look grey too and her reflection is a mere pencil-sketched outline watching her from the other side of the glass. The downpour surrounds her so she feels the swimmy sensation of being submerged. She feels damp and grey, as if the rain is seeping into her, dissolving her. She wonders, if she stands here long enough, will she gradually fade to nothingness and pool into a puddle on the tiles. Would she remain sentient if that is all she was? Would she be able to sense the cracks and crevices of the stone? How hard and cold would it feel under her liquid skin?

If she did dissolve all her component parts would remain. Because all matter goes on existing. She would be broken down to the tiniest fragments. Perhaps one day even the soul would be found to have a particle nature or something else which could be detected.

When Ambrose first looked for Dark Matter, she'd had a notion that he might find a particle and it would be named after him, like the Higgs boson was named for the scientist who theorised it. She would toss the words 'Ambrose' and 'Isherwood' in her mind to see which name she preferred. It is a comforting thought that tiny Ambrose and Isherwood, sub-atomic specks, might be with her always.

Her feet are bare and she presses each toe down to sense the upward pressure of the floor but her flesh is numb.

The house behind her is silent. No Ambrose. No Marietta. No hum and clatter. Even the grandfather clock remains dumb. A tiny thought hopes Norma will visit, breaking this enchantment with a 'Yoo Hoo'. But the house stays empty, inert and silent because there is NO SIMEON. He is lying in a stainless steel room, remote from the world. Kate imagines herself marooned in a similar place where everything has been sterilised, its essence removed.

A bell chimes repeatedly, gradually building to a noise that interrupts Kate's thoughts and she recognises as the front door bell. It rarely sounds; everybody who knows them comes to the back door. Having wished for an interruption to her loneliness Kate now feels agitated that a stranger, an interloper, should be standing on the doorstep. She walks slowly down the corridor hoping that the intruder might give up and go away. But instead the bell rings again. Kate can make out a tall shrouded shape behind the glass panels. A dark-hooded silhouette.

Her fingers feel cold as she fiddles with the lock and puts the chain across the door before she opens it. She can't help but gasp as she peers through the gap in the door because it is indeed the Grim Reaper standing before her. Tall and cloaked in a dark Mackintosh, eyes masked with dark glasses, shaking a hooked umbrella out. Kate is about to cry out, when a soft voice sounds from the red-lipped mouth just visible under the hood. 'Hi, sorry to bother you. It's Kate, isn't it? Is Ambrose in?'

Kate stares. Not the Grim Reaper but somebody she doesn't know, who recognises her.

'Oh, sorry, love,' the figure apologises, 'I'm Mallory, and it would be great if I could come in for a moment. I feel a bit exposed standing out here.' And she glances over her shoulder as if she expects to see a horde of people chasing her.

This is what finally makes Kate move her fingers to undo the catch and open the door.

She is the one apologising now, realising how foolish she must look. She repeats, 'Sorry,' several times and feels even more stupid. How could she fail to recognise this celebrity? She can see a reflection of herself in Mallory's dark glasses, a bowing and scraping fool. She wishes she had put some footwear on. Mallory looms over her. Kate looks at her pale feet with their yellowing nails and bunion bulge and thinks, 'I have old feet.' She doesn't have a clue what Mallory is thinking.

She manages a stuttered, 'I'm sorry; Ambrose isn't here at the moment. I'm not sure when he'll be back. Did you want to leave him a message?'

But this is the woman who had an assignation with Ambrose at the mine, which he failed to mention to her. The density of Mallory's shadow over her appears to deepen.

Mallory's umbrella is dripping water onto the tiles. Kate watches the drops coalesce into a stream.

'Oh, hell, I am so sorry,' says Mallory, noticing the direction of Kate's gaze. 'It's filthy out.'

Kate suddenly realises she has asked Mallory to come through to the kitchen to dry out. Somehow, she has Mallory's umbrella in her hand and looks at it as if it is an alien object. 'What am I supposed to do with this?' she asks herself, and hopes she hasn't spoken the words aloud. Finally she puts it in the gunroom.

'Would you like a cup of tea? I was just going to make one,' Kate asks, in a robotic voice. Why is she being so nice to this woman? This person who might be having an affair with Ambrose.

'Perhaps, if you have green tea?'

'I think so, somewhere.' Kate wonders if the green tea she finds in an old caddy at the back of the cupboard will be stale.

Once the tea is made, they sit opposite each other at the kitchen table. Kate cannot think of anything to say. Her brain is still numbed by the thought of Simeon in that impersonal stainless steel room and Mallory's presence barely impinges on that. But now the idea of Mallory and Ambrose together trembles in her temple, nudging her thoughts in waves of worry. She really cannot handle the idea of Ambrose's infidelity at this moment, but it is difficult to ignore. What if Simeon dies, and Ambrose leaves her, she would have nothing. Nothing. Her headache swells and she puts a hand to her brow.

'Are you alright?' Mallory asks, reaching over and touching Kate's arm. Kate realises she must have let out a whimper. She stares at Mallory's hand against her sleeve. The fingernails are perfectly painted with a French varnish, shiny on her unblemished skin, like hands in an advert. Her gaze moves down her own sleeve to the rough, red knuckles and veins of her own hands, and she shudders, wondering if she is transforming into a hag. She is reminded of the story of Sleeping Beauty, but the story has become grotesque.

'Let me get you a tissue,' Mallory says, removing her fingers from Kate's arm. She digs into a handbag and passes a folded tissue to Kate. Kate takes it and dabs her face, breathing in Mallory's fragrance, aware that her cheeks are wet with tears and her nose is sticky with snot. She needs to change the subject, and there is only one thing she can think of to say.

'You went to the mine with Ambrose?' It is less a question more a statement.

'Yeah, it was fab. So interesting,' Mallory pauses to sip her tea. 'People don't tend to take me seriously when it comes to science. You're a scientist too, aren't you?'

Kate watches Mallory as she lifts her cup to her lips in an elegant motion.

'Yes, though not in Ambrose's league. I do routine lab stuff for the university.'

'That's still so exciting, though. Did you meet Ambrose there?'

'No, we met when I was doing my post-grad studies in London. He was one of the tutors.' Kate realises she is blushing and looks down at her hands. It always makes her smile when she remembers how they clicked. It wasn't the simple lustful sensation people might call love at first sight, but there had definitely been a reaction which must have been rooted in a chemistry, because it felt so inevitable. When she looks up Mallory is smiling at her, 'He's a really good man, Ambrose. He was like a dad to me in the jungle.'

'Oh, I thought...' Kate begins but then realises she shouldn't say more.

'What, you thought we were getting together? Ha, that's funny. No way!' Mallory has tipped back in her chair so the screech of the chair legs on the tiles matches the squeal of incredulity in her voice. 'Sorry, don't mean to be rude but he's more like me dad's age.'

They regard each other across the table, sipping their teas, while the last sentence subsides.

Suddenly Mallory says, 'You have a son, don't you?' She looks around as if expecting a boy to materialise in a corner of the kitchen.

Kate feels a weight in her chest, making it difficult to breathe; she doesn't want to talk about this.

'Yes, Simeon. He's away tonight.'

'On a sleepover?'

Kate nods, wondering what it would be like if Simeon was merely staying at a friend's house for a night, rather than sleeping in a hospital bed at the lab. She gives out a small choked laugh. How many years of worry would she have had if Simeon had been an ordinary boy, doing normal things like sleepovers? And now it seems that all that fretting she had avoided has amassed to one gigantic climax, like a car crash.

# XVIII

The speck that has interested the entity radiates more strongly the closer it is examined. It pulses with potential. The nearer the entity sweeps, the faster it flows as if there is a pull which it has not comprehended before. The entity realises that it has created this, enabled this point. It might have purpose. It might be a salve.

Simeon hears a noise, it is unlike anything he has been aware of before but has the same insistence as a buzzer sounding in one of his school games. It demands a response. Instinctively he moves his arm. But he can't raise it. It is heavy and takes too much effort to lift. He tries again. Now it rises a millimetre and he is aware of the tug of pulleys as his arm jerks off the bed. It hurts. The noise changes, rises higher, as he moves his fingers, they tremble. 'Simeon' the voice repeats, 'Simeon, can you hear me?'

There is some familiarity with the 'Simeon' word. He starts to murmur in response. 'Mmm' he says. The voice crescendos.

'Simeon!' Kate shouts with excitement. She gazes round blindly for somebody to share the enormity of Simeon's response, to witness it with her. Nobody is there. Just cold white walls and steel cabinets reflecting her image, and Simeon's bed, so he appears to be floating.

Simeon does not know what he has done. The noise around him is frightening. His brain tells him to scream but when he opens his mouth other sound burbles out. 'Aaahh,' This hurts his throat and scares him more. 'Aaahh aaahh aaahh.' He tries to scream again, then perhaps everything will change to quietness; he will be able to *think*. His mouth feels strange, like a great hole that he has no control over. His jaw hurts, his face hurts.

Something is touching his arm. The voice has become quieter. 'Simeon, Hush. It's alright; it's going to be alright.'

This is better. The voice calms him. It is not demanding him to do anything.

Both Simeon and Kate are aware of an intrusion at the periphery of the room. 'I think that's enough for now, Mrs Isherwood. We don't want Simeon to become agitated. We must try to understand how strange this world is going to be to him.'

Kate knows this. She hates the patronising tone of the nurse.

# XIX

The pulse of the entity quickens as it realises the potential of a solar mass. A human with an illness might reach for the medicine bottle and take comfort from the bright round pill that will ease his pain. The entity views our Sun like that, a tablet of warmth. Nuclear reactions with the energy to help its child. In its dense interior atoms are colliding and fusing, creating colossal streams of energy and the potential to treat its patient.

'Well, are you going to tell me where Simeon is?'

Norma has dropped in. Having firstly asked where Simeon is, she has had to repeat the follow-up question three times and still neither Ambrose nor Kate has been able to reply. Kate is embarrassed. She wishes she'd had the courage to speak up before Simeon's operation. She tries to say something but her mouth won't work.

It is Ambrose who finally speaks. 'Simeon is in hospital, having a ground-breaking operation. It is going to change everything.'

Ambrose is reminded of a pufferfish as he watches Norma respond. She visibly swells, her mouth gurns as she spits out her words.

'Didn't you think to speak to me about this?' Her lips quiver as if trying to form an expletive strong enough to sum up her dismay. Finally she states, 'I am disgusted!'

Norma sounds like the head teacher she once was. Her outrage fills the kitchen and both Kate and Ambrose feel shrunken by its force. Ambrose is remembering being slippered by his headmaster. Norma's words make a similar sting against his skin. Just as he did those many years ago, he knows he must remain calm and not reveal his distress.

'And has this thing actually happened?'

'Yes, and Simeon is responding very well. In fact he's due back home next week. You'd be welcome to come over and see him then. See what a positive step this is.'

Norma makes a sound that is unintelligible; a spittle-filled growl, full of venom.

'I'll leave you to it. My opinion on this matter is obviously worthless to you.' She turns and slams the kitchen door as she departs. Kate has the urge to run after her, apologise.

She takes two steps then stops, realising the futility of this idea.

Still facing the door she says, 'We should have told her. I should say sorry.'

'We had the opportunity to tell her,' Ambrose says. 'We chose not to tell her. Probably because we knew her reaction would be unreasonable.'

'But she's still my mother. I should have said something.'

Ambrose steps behind Kate and puts his hand on her shoulder, he senses Kate shudder beneath his fingers. 'What's done is done. The most important thing is that the surgery has been a success.'

Kate looks at the squares indenting the door, and notices the lines of dust along the ledges. She must speak to Marietta about it. Or perhaps she won't. She reaches out her hand and rubs her index finger along the wood, lifting the grey particles onto her skin. She recalls that dust mainly comprises skin cells shed from humans. The debris on her finger contains elements of her, Ambrose and Simeon. The old Simeon. She rubs her fingers together feeling the slippery substance coat the tips, retaining the essence of a previous existence. She contemplates finding a small vial and bottling all the dust in the house. 'What's done is done,' she hears an echo of Ambrose's recent words, but what have they done? She is crying and Ambrose has managed to turn her and enfold her in his arms. 'It's going to be alright,' he says, but he utters it like a mantra, just words which should be said. The phrase does not sound true even to his own ears.

# XX

The entity moves in silence. There will be no warning if it alters its shape to drown the earth in a different dimension. We will not sense it if it decides to remove the sun. We will not hear it coming, however many microphones or probes we litter space with. If we are fortunate, we will gather tell tale specks trailing in its wake.

'Simeon, catch the ball.' Something thuds beside Simeon. 'Let's try again shall we? Can we remember how I showed you?'

Simeon is sitting in a chair; the catching exercise seems to have been going on for a long time. It is alright when Alison lifts his arms and places the ball in his hands but when she throws it towards him his limbs won't lift. He knows what to do; he just can't make it happen. His arms won't respond to his internal commands. Another thud sounds beside him.

'Come on now, let's try again shall we?' He can hear the sigh as Alison crouches beside his chair. A rush of warm air is exhaled into his ear. This is an occurrence he is learning very quickly. Disappointment. This sensation is already wired into his frame, he has experienced it before when his body is asked to do things and he has been unable to perform.

'Put your hands around the ball like this', Alison places his palms on the leathery cover of the ball, 'Then you have to watch it carefully. Shall we try again?'

Simeon wants to say 'No', but his vocal chords haven't learnt to work yet, so all that comes out is a 'Ungh'.

'Yes. That's great.'

This time the ball lands in his lap and, although Simeon has not done anything different, Alison enthuses, 'Well done, that's better.'

Kate has come in quietly. She watches from the edge of the room and observes her son put through training like a performing seal. At any moment she expects him to clap his hands together.

Alison seeing Kate says, 'Look whose here, Simeon. Shall we do a really good one for Mummy?'

Simeon waits for the thump of the ball again, knowing he has no chance of catching it.

'I think you're getting tired, aren't you?' Alison walks across the room; Simeon can hear her footsteps slap against the wood of the floor. In his peripheral vision he can see Alison's figure blur, talking to another being, which he realises is the person called, 'Mummy'. This name seems to hold huge significance for everyone, but she is just another indistinct shape that regularly swims into his field of vision. His sight is still not very good, so objects fly towards him like shadows and then solidify in front of him. Faces loom up and it takes time for him to put the pixelated pieces into an order that he can recognise. It makes him dizzy. There are always people about. He is never alone any more. Wherever he is, figures will emerge out of the atmosphere around him. He is never quite ready for them.

Simeon hears, 'He's doing very well,' and then indistinct words between the physiotherapist and Mummy. He does not feel he is doing well. He does not feel well at all.

This morning it was walking. He had to grasp poles on either side of him and struggle between them, until he crumpled. His whole body aches. Even his brain aches, it is so full of new information and instruction. His face is wet, and he recognises that he is crying. This is something that happens frequently, he does not understand why. He does not know how to stop it.

# XXI

The complexity of the entity cannot be underestimated; it permeates everything, from before the beginning to after the end. It pervades all dimensions. It holds everything together, yet keeps them apart. It is at the centre but encompasses the whole. It is both cause and effect.

Meltdown. That's how Kate would describe it. Again she has woken in a slick of sweat, emerging from dreams of flames. Outside it is raining heavily or possibly hailing. The hiss and spark pelts the windowpane filling her head with hammers. She imagines herself in a forge being re-shaped. Her limbs ache as if being twisted. She recalls the 'growing pains' she'd experienced as a child when, on waking, her legs would be tired as if she'd been running all night. Her body appears to be going through another metamorphosis. She thinks of Ambrose's hills and wonder if they hurt as they transform. And now Simeon; is he experiencing anything similar as he emerges from a disabled child into someone else. The tale of *Pinocchio* comes into her head and she strokes the wood of the bed frame imagining the rending that would occur if wood changed into flesh. Was Simeon going through a similar conversion? She groans at the thought that all change suffers an accompanying distress, whether at birth, adolescence, pregnancy or menopause. Even her virginity had been ripped from her in a drunken grope in darkness; barely consented. The step between girl and womanhood just another tear in the fabric of her existence. Perhaps it is only with death that trauma ceases as the final change occurs. But life is a continuous alteration from birth to death so the whole of life is endured with pain.

As yet, she is not privy to Simeon's situation. His speech is coming on but remains monosyllabic. She still has difficulty differentiating between the 'Ugh' for 'Yes' and the 'Ungh' for 'No'. Worse is the 'Mu' for 'Mum' or the 'Ma' for 'Marietta', it reminds her of the days of the 'Mmm' arguments of old. And in Kate's perception, his preference remains for Marietta.

Ambrose left for work hours ago. His departure seems to be getting earlier each day, leaving all of Simeon's care to her and Marietta. She hadn't thought it would be like this, where she is responsible for the bulk of his convalescence. Kamir has given her time off work, but sometimes she craves the idea of getting out, escaping from the post of nursemaid. The thought of checking data and looking down a microscope is now more appealing.

Kate hears creaking floorboards along the corridor and turns over, trying not to feel guilt. She will let Marietta deal with Simeon this morning, after all that's why they invited Marietta to live in for a time. But sometimes it feels as if Marietta has taken over the house. A trail of her scent prevails wherever she has been so Kate feels as if she is following her movements all the time. Marietta also carries a halo of godliness with her, and again Kate wonders how a God could let humans exist in such torment.

Marietta shuffles down the corridor; the air is always cold in this large house. The sash windows let in draughts and rattle with constant background menace. Chilly air follows at her ankles, nipping like a terrier. She stares accusingly at the closed door to the Isherwoods' bedroom thinking, 'She really should be up by now'.

Shaking her head, she progresses downstairs to Simeon's room and knocks on the door. She waits for a moment on the threshold and smiles at Simeon's small figure curved under the covers. His eyes are open and he is staring at the ceiling. But now, instead of a glassy stare and fitful body movement, the eyes are filled with animation and the limbs restful. Under her breath she murmurs, 'Thank God. Thank God he's alright.'

'Good morning, my love,' she says, 'What a beautiful morning to be alive.' And she flings the curtains aside, making the rings clatter along the rail. Grey light fills the room.

Simeon is already awake. He has been listening to the various noises of the house and the sound of rain striking the window. Traffic hums in the distance. Closer, heating pipes clang, and the house creaks. These are noises he has a vague recollection of, but now they vibrate and throb more loudly. As they whir around him he feels isolated and abandoned within a cascade of sound from which he has no escape. Once his body would have ebbed and flowed with the background sounds and he would have felt at one with the energy that surged through him, in harmony with the universe. Now, the bark of a dog or screech of a bird snap at his nerve endings. The effect is so harsh that he is constantly trembling. Now he has an itch on his shoulder, it needles him but he is unable to reach to scratch it. As he thinks about it the irritation increases, making him whimper. As Marietta draws the curtains back the light is hard and the movement of raindrops so vivid he has to close his eyes.

'Don't screw your eyes up, little man; look at the beautiful day God has given us. We must make the most of it.'

Simeon feels the tap of Marietta's fingers on his head, he crouches smaller and screws his eyes more tightly. Her fingers strike him as if the rain has breached the glass. He is shaking, anxiety overtaking his senses. In a moment he knows he will have to get up and get dressed, asked to do things he finds difficult and painful. He does not want to do anything. Coiled under his bedclothes he starts to cry.

'Now, now Simeon. Don't get upset. We'll go out today. I've got a special treat for you'.

Marietta can't understand why Simeon cries so much of the time. Before the operation he was always grinning and gurgling. She thought he would enjoy being at home rather than in the sterile confines of the hospital. He has been doing so well, starting to walk and talk and eat, just like a regular boy. She supposes it will take time for him to adjust, he is like a toddler getting used to a new home.

The wind is blowing straight into Simeon's face, he feels it whipping at his skin. The wheelchair is uncomfortable, not like his old chair with straps and contours, this one makes him sit upright and it has a thin seat so he suffers every bump on the path.

Finally, after the traumatic ride, where the outside world has clashed and clanged about him in a terrifying tumult, Simeon has arrived at a place of calm. His eyes have adjusted to the dim atmosphere. The light is beautifully muted with a faint colouration. The smell is comforting too, warm and inviting, something that stirs familiar memories from long ago, from a place he felt safe.

'This is the Church, Simeon,' Marietta tells him in a whisper, 'This is God's house'.

Simeon does not who God is. Perhaps it is another person he must meet. A figure who will ask him, 'How are you feeling?' A question for which he has no answer. He has no words to explain his condition, just that his head feels full and heavy. Images and words flit and fly around trying to make connections. His thoughts won't support his body movements and his limbs are weak and clumsy. He is choked by new sensations. But now he breathes in deeply. God's house smells nice, a familiar odour which clings to his hair and skin. He can taste it on his tongue, sense it swelling in his chest and feels calmer.

'Shall we light a candle?'

Marietta holds Simeon's hand on a taper to flick a new flame to life. Simeon lets out a little noise, 'Eeh,' with the thrill and surprise as the fire prances. He wants to make it happen again but his guttural invocations only make Marietta say, 'Oh, you want to say a prayer, don't you? Let me show you how to pray.'

Simeon listens as Marietta holds his palms together and advises on the rudiments of a prayer. 'Our Father, who art in heaven...'

Simeon thinks the words pleasant as they sound lyrical in his head, but they are not distinguishable from all the other noises and words he has heard before, playing rhythmically through his life, when he used to sit and converse with the universe without pain.

With her hands around his, Marietta experiences only delight that she can share God's wonder with Simeon. She is so moved there are tears in her eyes. There is only one remaining niggle, so she adds a silent prayer and 'Hail Mary' to assuage her guilt at lying to Mrs Isherwood. She had told her she was taking Simeon to the park.

Kate is sitting at the kitchen table, waiting for the door to open, for the sound of Simeon and Marietta's return. She has nothing to do except wait. All the build up to the operation has gone, like water down a plughole, leaving her so empty that she feels constantly nauseous. She is still waiting but now there is no fixed event to concentrate on. No end point. It is two months since the operation but during that interval time appears to have warped. When Kate reflects on her life, events appear jumbled; she has difficulty acknowledging she is fifty and a mother because she feels as if she is still adolescent trying to come to terms with the world.

At the click of the door she lifts her head and fixes a smile on her face. But it is Norma who comes into the room. There is no accompanying 'Yoo Hoo'. Her mother has not visited for weeks.

'I thought I'd better come and check how you were doing?' she says. Though dressed, Kate hasn't put any make-up on and she wonders how long it will be before Norma comments on this.

'I'll put the kettle on then, shall I?' Norma asks.

Kate watches her mother make the unfamiliar walk to fill the kettle and get cups out of the cupboard. She comes and sits at the table, and places two mugs of coffee down. She pats Kate's hand as she sits. 'Now my girl, how's Simeon getting on?'

'Marietta's taken him out,' Kate mumbles, 'He's okay.'

'So the operation has been a success?'

'Yes', Kate intones, but the word is too small to accommodate exactly what the surgery achieved. Kate is realising that Simeon will never be the boy she once dreamed of. The perfect child.

# XXII

The entity is nearly ready. With what humanity might call motion, it will use the power of the Sun to heal its child. Then it will turn away.

It is still dark when Ambrose leaves the house. His feet crunch, leaving footprints on a scatter of frosted snow. He knows they will quickly be obliterated by a new fall of flakes, it saddens him to think about what will be lost under the fresh cover. He can't help but apply a similar sense of loss to Simeon. He starts the car and sits while it warms up, watching as a few snowflakes drift onto the windscreen. Thoughts of sledging and snowball fights with Simeon hover and then melt away. He is tired. When he is at home the atmosphere is like mercury, he constantly feels he is pushing through liquid. He assumed this part would be simpler, that Simeon's recovery would be straightforward. His hands grip the steering wheel; the knuckles protrude like ranges of pale hills.

The snow is falling harder now and he flicks the wiper to arc through the covering. He tries to remember an equation for the mathematical construction of a snowflake, and immediately feels calmer. The rules of algebra are predictable, constant; unlike human behaviour and development. As he drives out of the gate he is almost singing mathematical logarithms like an old familiar song, which makes a long journey more bearable.

Simeon's head already aches when he wakes, as if his mind has been busy all night, constructing his new world. As his eyelids flick open allowing the stab of light to accost his eyes he knows it will begin; the regiment of another day. He knows when he rises there will be no peace. He wants to curl up in a ball under his bedclothes, remaining in half-light. Outside the illumination is so bright it engulfs his room, making him feel tiny and vulnerable. The air is cold.

He wants to retreat back to the calm, silent world he used to dwell in. A being in his own corner of the universe, with nothing expected of him.

Simeon has to get himself up now; he stumbles as he moves and struggles with his clothes. He enters the kitchen already shell shocked by the day's activities. Kate stares at him as he spoons cereal into his mouth, watching milk dribble down his chin. She knows she must not help him. 'He has to learn to do these tasks himself,' she has been told over and over by the medical team. 'It will get easier,' they tell her. But it is not easy because every time he achieves one activity there is another thing he must learn. Kate recalls days that seem so long ago when she fed him porridge and wiped his face and questions whether life was more difficult then or now. Things are different. That is all.

On the timetable following breakfast, Simeon must do exercises Alison has given him to strengthen his fingers. Kate has handed Simeon a yellow ball and he is squeezing it in his fist. He has to lift each digit and then replace it one by one like performing scales on a keyboard. There is no music in this task. Kate knows she has dreamt about this ball, or a ball like it. She has watched a fist close around the orb, not Simeon's fist, not any fist she has ever seen; pressing and squeezing so that the yellow globe shatters to dust.

Now Simeon drops the ball, this happens a lot. It rumbles across the floor. He will have to bend down and pick it up which will take time and effort. Simeon is not sure he can be bothered.

He manages to clamber out of his chair; the electric motor whirring the seat to eject him forward. Using sticks he hobbles over the floor, his legs dragging. As he moves he stumbles and his foot touches the ball, sending it rolling away.

Kate watches him as he struggles. Her muscles pull in a reciprocal effort as she not only fights to help him but also

106

restrain herself from running forward to assist. She has been told not to interfere by both the physio and occupational therapists. She presses her fingertips into her palms, the nails digging into the flesh and she bites her lip.

Simeon knows he is being watched. He touches the ball again and it rolls further away. Each movement takes so much effort he is already tired. Slowly he sinks down onto the floor. He is crying again.

Kate rushes forward. She helps Simeon to his feet, returns him to his chair and picks the ball up. Simeon takes it and continues his finger exercises. Neither will say anything about the intervention. Kate won't record it on the daily progress chart. The report will remain unblemished.

As Kate returns to her chair she flicks the television on, grateful for the distraction of a daytime soap; characters who aren't real; selected parts of their lives revealed and other parts ignored, their existence in limbo between one scene and the next.

At the click of the switch, Simeon looks up. The image fizzes into life but he can't focus on the screen. Pixels of light accost him from across the room like a swarm of flies buzzing into his brain. They permeate every sense, irritating his nose making him want to sneeze. He can't sneeze so the pressure builds making his sinuses swell and ache. In the back of his throat his saliva tastes gritty and bitter. Tears sting his eyes and his ears perceive a high-pitched screech. His heart races accompanying the whirring sound with cracks like glass shattering. His head hurts, every part of his being hurts. He clenches his fist around the yellow ball, the tendons stretching across his knuckles, painful with the movement. He wants the agitation to stop. He wants his pain to stop. To stop!

The entity has moved into position. The solar medication, which will cure its child, is here. You will not hear the tearing of space, the swirling of dimension and matter as our laws of physics are shattered, but you may sense something, a hint of change in the air as if a terrible storm were approaching, the tremor and throb of a tornado gathering speed, sweeping everything before it, sucking up the matter of space. You might be afraid, and not know why, as your skin prickles and your head aches. The entity does not have hands but, as a metaphor, consider it does. Imagine, if you will, an unclenched fist, palm up. Now watch it closing. In that fist observe a fiery yellow orb. Imagine the fingers concealing our Sun.

Then life on earth will cease.
Nothing will remain except a black hole.
Nothing will remain except a black hole filled with dark matter.

**Stephanie Percival** always intended to write a novel, but it wasn't until 2004 when she was shortlisted for the BBC End of Story competition, that she believed it might be possible. That was the motivation to develop, *The Memory of Wood*, and self-publish it in 2011.

She has continued to write and was shortlisted in the Writers and Artists short story competition, 2013 with 'You promised me a mocking bird', and won the Firewords short story competition in 2016, with 'The man with no shadow'.

*The Kim's Game*, which was long-listed in the Cinnamon Press Debut Novel Competition, was published in October 2017.

Stephanie is a member of the Creative Writers @ Museum, in Northampton. They meet regularly and use the exhibits as stimulation for their work, producing portfolios to accompany the exhibitions.

She works as a podiatrist for her local NHS service. She lives in Northamptonshire with her husband, Adrian, and has three children, Nick, Alistair and Katie.

You can connect with Stephanie on Facebook: StephaniePercival—Author, or on her website: www.stephaniepercival.com